SOMETHING WIKI

SUZANNE SUTHERLAND

SOMETHING **WIKI**

SUZANNE SUTHERLAND

DUNDURN
TORONTO

Editor: Shannon Whibbs
Design: Laura Boyle
Cover Design: Crysta Horner
Cover images © chihhang/ LeeDaniels
Printer: Webcom

Library and Archives Canada Cataloguing in Publication

Sutherland, Suzanne, 1987-, author
    Something wiki / Suzanne Sutherland.

Issued in print and electronic formats.

ISBN 978-1-4597-2821-9 (pbk.).--ISBN 978-1-4597-2822-6 (pdf).--
ISBN 978-1-4597-2823-3 (epub)

    I. Title.
PS8637.U865S64 2014   jC813'.6   C2014-902122-4
                                               C2014-902123-2

    2   3   4   5   19   18   17   16   15

  Canadä

We acknowledge the support of the **Canada Council for the Arts** and the **Ontario Arts Council** for our publishing program. We also acknowledge the financial support of the **Government of Canada** through the **Canada Book Fund** and **Livres Canada Books**, and the **Government of Ontario** through the **Ontario Book Publishing Tax Credit** and the **Ontario Media Development Corporation**.

Care has been taken to trace the ownership of copyright material used in this book. The author and the publisher welcome any information enabling them to rectify any references or credits in subsequent editions.

J. Kirk Howard, President

Visit us at
Dundurn.com | *@dundurnpress* | *Facebook.com/dundurnpress* | *Pinterest.com/dundurnpress*

Dundurn
3 Church Street, Suite 500
Toronto, Ontario, Canada
M5E 1M2

Gazelle Book Services Limited
White Cross Mills
High Town, Lancaster, England
L41 4XS

Dundurn
2250 Military Road
Tonawanda, NY
U.S.A. 14150

For my parents, Lynn and Walt
And my cool older brother, Sam

ONE

Acne vulgaris

From Wikipedia, the free encyclopedia (*as edited by me*)

Acne vulgaris (or cystic acne, *a.k.a. looking like a total greaseball*) is a ~~common~~ *pretty nasty* human skin disease, characterized by areas of skin with seborrhea (scaly red skin — *ew*), comedones (blackheads and whiteheads — *sick*), papules (pinheads — *gross*), pustules (pimples — *duh*), nodules (large papules — *which sounds like some kind of walrus*), and possibly scarring *(oh, great)*.

There was a commercial that used to play on TV a lot when I was little. I mean, when I was really little. I was pretty much a newborn, just sleeping, eating, and wearing diapers. This was back when my older brother was the same age I am now, which is twelve — thirteen in a couple of months, in March. He used to tape-record a lot of shows on TV, which is what people did back in the Stone Age if they wanted to watch something more than once. Zim says the nineties were not the Stone Age, and that he's not that old. Zim's my brother, and he is that old. He's twice as old as I am, twenty-four.

A lot of people think it's weird that my brother is so much older than me. Zim would say that a lot of those people are pretty weird themselves.

Zim is short for Zimmerman.

As in Robert Allen Zimmerman, which is Bob Dylan's real name.

As in, who the heck is Bob Dylan?

As in, some craggy-faced old folk singer who my parents love.

Or, in the wise words of Wiki: an American singer-songwriter, musician, author and artist. He has been an influential figure in popular music and culture for over five decades.

His voice is weird, but his songs are actually pretty good.

Anyway, Zim doesn't live at home anymore, which is okay. Our house is pretty small, and there really isn't room for more than three people in it. Zim has his own apartment downtown that he shares with his roommate, whose name is Swirly. Mom says their apartment smells like pepperoni and toxic waste. She says their neighbourhood, Parkdale, is "kind of seedy," and she wishes they could afford to live somewhere nicer. But Zim says that rent downtown is expensive, so I guess they can't afford to live anywhere else.

I still haven't been there, to the Parkdale Pepperoni/ Toxic Waste Dump. I'm not even sure if Swirly is Zim's roommate's real name. It's probably not. His real name's probably Kevin or Mike or Mark or something. Something boring. I mean, who would seriously name their kid Swirly? Then again, who would seriously name their kid Zimmerman?

My parents named me Jo, after Jo March from *Little Women*. Sometimes I wonder why my parents couldn't just come up with their own names for Zim and me, instead of ripping off a jagged old folkie and a fictional character from the 1800s, which actually was the Stone Age. Sometimes I wonder what my life would be like if I hadn't been named after a figment of some writer's imagination.

Zim says he'll invite me over one day, to his and Swirly/Kevin-Mike-Mark's apartment. Well, once he said it. He said it once. He said we'd hang out with his girlfriend, Jen (short for Jenevieve, not Jennifer), and the three of us would order Thai food and watch movies and stay up so late we'd see the sun come up. He said that he and J would show me around downtown, that I'd get to see all the cool little shops and cafés where they hang out. I'd even get to see the record store where Zim works, which he swears is just like this movie called *Empire Records* (I watched it on Netflix once, it's about this bunch of slackers who save the record store where they work from corporate destruction).

I'd like that, to spend more time with Zim and Jen, and to see the city the way they do.

No, scratch that. I'd *love* to hang out with Z and J (which is what I call them in my head, but never say out loud) and pretend, for even an afternoon, that I live in their world. I've only met Jen, J, once, but she is unbelievably beautiful and completely cool. Her hair was bright purple then, when she came over to our house for Thanksgiving, but Z says she dyes it a different colour practically every other week. Z's hair is always the same colour, though. Dirty blond, usually actually dirty, and also usually hanging in his eyes. J works at a bookstore downtown, and when she came over for Thanksgiving she brought me this amazing graphic novel about a group of girls who are all named Jane and who make radical public art in their neighbourhood. I'd never seen a comic book — or any book, really — like that before, and I was totally blown away. How did J even know I would like something like that? You can see why I'd love to spend more time with her.

I'm dying for Z to have me over, but he only ever mentioned it that one time, and that was almost a year ago. Mom says I have to wait to be invited to his apartment, I can't just ask to visit; it would be rude. I think she'd be just as happy if I didn't hang out downtown. I don't think she's nuts about Swirly/Kevin-Mike-Mark. Or J, really.

Anyway, I wasn't talking about Z, or S/K-M-M, or J and her hair, or my parents, I was talking about this TV commercial.

I get distracted sometimes. Okay, a lot. I get distracted a lot.

I spend a lot of time online, whole hours and some-times days, just looking stuff up — weird stuff, stupid stuff, boring stuff, whatever.

My deep, dark secret? I edit Wikipedia for fun (I know, I know). I put in goofy stuff that only makes sense to me, private jokes and little stories about my day. I've never told anyone about what I do — my friends and family already think I'm enough of a dork without me telling them that I use an online encyclo-pedia for a diary. So I put all my ideas and feelings out there online, everything I'm thinking and won-dering about, and then some other geek in some other corner of cyberspace a million miles away sees what I've done and deletes it. Usually pretty quickly, too. We geeks work fast. But there's something weirdly satisfy-ing about putting my words out into the universe only to have them disappear in a split second, totally erased. It feels like I'm writing out my secrets in the sand on a beach. Eventually the waves will carry everything back to the water, and all I'll be left with is the memory of the words.

What was I talking about again?

Right, the commercial. So this commercial used to come on pretty much every ten minutes in between the shows Z taped. He watched stuff like *Saved by the Bell*, which is about teenagers who pretend to be serious some of the time, but mostly just act like idiots. There's this one episode where a girl named Jessie takes a cou-ple of caffeine pills 'cause she's stressing out about mid-terms and having to perform that dumb song "I'm So

Excited" and the pills make her flip out and cry. I some-how doubt that popping a few over-the-counter pills would make you that sick. Z says he practically lived on Red Bull while he was in university and he turned out fine.

I'm not kidding about the commercial, though; this thing played all the time, you couldn't miss it. When I got a bit older and I started watching Z's tapes, I started seeing this commercial practically every day. When I was little we were the only family in the neighbourhood that still had a VCR, which is what you use to play video tapes. VCRs make a lot of noise, and you have to rewind the tape before you can watch it again from the beginning and that takes forever. I don't know what VCR stands for, but I bet wonderful Wikipedia does.

We finally got a DVD player when I was eight, about a million years after everybody else did. But I still like watching tapes sometimes, even if I do have to rewind them when I'm finished.

It drives my parents crazy that I can't tell a story straight through from the beginning to the end, but it's not that I don't try. It's just that sometimes I think the funny little moments in between are more interesting than the big ending.

Like sometimes when I read a book, even if it's one I really like, I don't read all the way to the end. I could probably guess what's going to happen most of the time anyway. And besides, if I don't get to the end, the book is still kind of alive for me. The story isn't finished yet.

But that has nothing to do with this story I'm telling now. At least I don't think it does.

I'm going to try one more time.

I am. I *am*.

… I forgot what I was going to say.

TWO

Absent-mindedness

From Wikipedia, the free encyclopedia

Absent-mindedness is where a person shows inattentive or forgetful behaviour. It can have three different causes:

1. a low level of attention ("blanking" or "zoning out") — *huh? what?*

2. intense attention to a single object of focus (hyperfocus — *hyper? who's hyper?*) that makes a person oblivious to events around him or her; or

3. unwarranted distraction of attention from the object of focus by irrelevant thoughts or environmental events *like everything about being twelve.*

Oh, right, the commercial. Duh.

The commercial is about a boy. It's about a boy with these giant crimson zits that're practically pulsating all over his face. He's got massive, disgusting pimples from his chin to his forehead.

They're everywhere.

Everywhere.

It's gross.

And he's talking about how people don't see him for who is, how they only see his acne. He's looking right at the camera and he says, "People think that I eat too many chocolate bars, or that I don't wash my face." But he's got this accent, I don't know what kind, and it sounds kinda sad but mostly just silly.

Later, I found the clip on YouTube and sent it to all my friends. It was pretty popular, it already had like a hundred thousand views. I guess I wasn't the only one who thought it was funny.

At Stacey's tenth birthday party that year, her mom put out bowls of red and pink Smarties. Stacey's birthday is February 13, so her parties always wind up being kind of Valentine's Day-ish. Anyway, Trisha licked a couple of the Valentine's Smarties and stuck them to her cheeks and said, "Pee-pull theenk I eat too men-y choc-o-lit bars." She sounded just like the commercial and it was hilarious. We all laughed so hard. Chloe even peed her pants a little, which made us all laugh even harder. But then Chloe got mad because she said we were making fun of her. We weren't really, but when you're stuffed to the brim with chocolate and ice cream cake and Doritos at one of your best friend's birthday parties, and one of your other friends is angry like a cartoon character with smoke coming out of her ears 'cause she's just peed her pants, it's pretty hard to stop laughing.

Mom brought tea tree oil home yesterday for my face. She said that she'd picked it up at the health food store down the street from where she works and that the girl who sold it to her had raved about how good it was and how well it had worked on her skin.

"I think we need to treat your skin organically," she said. "I read this article about holistic acne treatment and it had some really great ideas."

And then I thought about the commercial and wondered if this meant I wasn't going to be allowed to eat chocolate ever again, so I took the little bottle from her and went up to my room before she could tell me any more about how, according some magazine she picked up in her doctor's waiting room, munching on wheatgrass was going to solve all my problems.

Not that I have that many problems.

I know how lucky I am, really.

Most of the time.

I went on Facebook and saw that Trisha was online. We chatted a bit about school and stuff and I asked her how her piano practising was going. I knew she had a big exam coming up. She said it was fine, but that she was really getting bored of the pieces her teacher made her play.

>**Me:** What would you rather be doing?
>**Trisha:** Anything but Für Elise.
>**Me:** I had to google that. You're really playing Beethoven?

Trisha: Yeah, it's not that hard.

Me: We should start a band.

Trisha: Uh-huh, and what do you play?

Me: I could totally get my brother to teach me guitar. I don't think it's that hard.

Trisha: When's the last time you saw your brother?

Me: His birthday.

Trisha: Yeah, and when was that?

Me: … a couple months ago.

After that I made up an excuse and logged off. I like Trisha and everything, but she can be kind of blunt, like she doesn't realize she's being mean. Well, not mean exactly, but not nice, either. I don't know, it's complicated.

THREE

Friends (disambiguation)

From Wikipedia, the free encyclopedia

Friends is a United States television sitcom.

Friends or Friend may also refer to: partners in friendship, an interpersonal relationship between humans.

I have three friends. Do you think that's enough?

Stacey and I have been friends since grade two, and I don't really know how I existed before that. I mean, sure, there were girls in my class who'd sometimes invite me over after school, and there was a boy who used to live in the house next door who'd come over sometimes and play Batman with me, but I was never really close to anyone until I met Stacey. She is so pretty, and I always make her laugh. We were best friends right away, like magic.

Okay, okay, that was corny. But it's true, you know?

We've spent almost every day together since.

Then, in grade five, we met Trisha and Chloe when we were all in Ms. Dowling's class together. Ms. Dowling assigned the four of us to the same desk group on the first day. She'd arranged the whole class alphabetically, so Somerville (Chloe), Van Allsburg (Stacey), Waller (me), and Wynn (Trisha) were all together in the corner by the window. Stacey and I were glad to be sitting together, but the four of us all smiled nervously at each other as we took our seats that Monday morning. It didn't take long for Chloe and Trisha to catch up with all our inside jokes, though, and by Friday afternoon Ms. Dowling had to split us all up into different groups because she couldn't stop us from talking (and singing, and telling bad jokes and laughing so hard that we made Trisha snort). And we've all been best friends ever since.

Although Stacey's still my best-best friend.

Even though I'd never tell Trisha or Chloe.

Stacey's definitely the prettiest of my friends, but she's not a snob about it. She reads a lot. She owns the complete works of Jane Austen and the Brontë sisters. She practically has *Wuthering Heights* memorized. Which Brontë wrote that again?

Anyway, Stacey wears glasses, like me, but she's the kind of girl who could be cast in a bad teen movie about a nerd who gets a makeover and is suddenly crowned prom queen. The second she takes off her specs it's clear that Stacey could be walking runways in a few years if she wanted to. She says she's got too much of a brain to want to be a model (her older sister Becca is already represented by some super exclusive agency, but so far she's only been in a couple of cereal commercials), but she also owns more makeup than the rest of my friends combined.

Which isn't actually saying that much.

Unless you count the ever-growing collection of zit cover-up creams I've accumulated in the last few months. Stacey can't go shopping without insisting I try something new. We go to the drugstore together after school, and it goes like this: she tells me how great some new cover-up looks and that I have to buy it. I buy it with the tiny bit of allowance money I have, put it on once, and then vow to never wear it again. Who knew there were so many shades of fake-and-bake orange and pale-as-a-ghost white? My zits are a determined bunch, though, and they refuse to be covered up, camouflaged, or otherwise ignored.

I still love hanging out with Stacey, though. We're completely different, but I think that's what makes us such good friends.

If Stacey's the prettiest, then Chloe's got to be the smartest. She's also the most natural leader of our group, and, to be honest, sometimes she's kind of bossy. She's a real only child — unlike me, who only gets to pretend to be one when Z forgets to call home for weeks on end.

We're all smart, but I think Chloe's such a genius because her parents treat her like an adult. She doesn't have us over to her house very often, though. She's always talking about new stuff her parents have bought for their house, so I guess they're rich, or at least richer than my family.

As far as looks go, Chloe's a few baby steps ahead of me. She's got a nice face with good skin, but she gets teased a lot because of her ginger hair. The grade eight boys are really mean sometimes. I don't get it: don't they have anything better to do than make fun of someone's hair? But her locks are literally jack-o'-lantern orange, curled tight like miniature Slinkys, so I guess they attracts attention. She's tall too, like Stacey. They're both taller than most of the boys in our class. But Chloe's not skinny like Stacey. She's not fat, she's just kind of big. My dad calls her the Linebacker when he thinks I can't hear him. My parents never seem to notice how much sound travels in our house.

Trisha's the other shorty in our group, we're both five-foot-nothing. Trisha looks a bit younger than the rest of us. Let's just say that if there was a race for boobs in our group, she'd be losing (and Stacey would be in the lead). She's also half-Chinese. Our school is mostly white, but I'm not sure why that is.

Trisha gets kind of obsessed with things sometimes. I think she spends even more time on her computer than I do, which seems almost impossible. She listens to a lot of music that way, checking out bands that are playing in town even though we're too young to ever go to the shows. The library in our neighbourhood has a collection of local bands' CDs, and Trisha told me that that's how she first got into a lot of what she listens to. Who knew that libraries were such a breeding ground for secret rock and roll rebels? Not me.

And what about me? I'm the chunky geek with glasses that always seem to be smudged, wearing ancient hand-me-downs from Z's old closet, topped off with messy, brown, blah-boring hair. I'm not the prettiest or the smartest or the one with secret rocker dreams. I'm the one most likely to be tapped as a natural oil reserve. But at least I've got my sunny personality to keep me warm at night. Ha.

I checked Wikipedia again a little while after I edited the entry on friends.

It said:

> I have three friends. Do you think that's enough?
> *Of course not. Loser.*

And even though I knew it was just some troll who'd written it — someone who didn't know anything about me or my friends — it still kind of stung.

Later that night, just before bed, I decided to put the tea tree oil to the test.

I pulled my hair back out of my face with an elastic and twisted the cap off the little brown bottle marked ORGANIC ESSENTIAL OIL: TEA TREE. The stuff stank. Like, seriously. It stunk. The bathroom smelled like I was in the middle of some dank, tropical jungle with giant, hulking trees oozing hippie nectar all over me. The smell made me gag and then I started coughing so loudly that Dad had to bust down the door to make sure I wasn't choking to death.

"Cough it out!" he yelled. "Just keep coughing, Jo, you're going to be okay."

I swear I could hear excitement in his voice. Like the first aid course he'd signed himself up for last summer was finally going to pay off.

I shook my head hard back and forth, but he didn't seem to get the message: that I wasn't actually choking.

"You're going to be fine, sweetheart, just cough it out! Keep on coughing, come on!"

He was clapping his hands now, my own personal cheering section, with a look of parental concern on his face. A weird, worried cheerleader.

I finally caught my breath and blurted out, "No, Dad, it's not —" I coughed again. "It's — the oil."

"Oil?" he said, looking frantically around the cramped bathroom for the offending substance. "What oil?"

"The stuff —" I gasped, "Mom brought home."

"What?" he said, picking the little bottle up off the counter. "This stuff?"

"Yeah," I said. "That stuff," I breathed out hard, "is nasty."

And then Dad spent about an hour laughing at me. "Gale," he called, when he'd finally calmed himself to a giggle, "I don't think Jo's ready for this hippie hoodoo quite yet. We better stick to the drugstore." And then he started laughing again. Which I'm sure really did wonders for my self-esteem.

FOUR

Sleepover

From Wikipedia, the free encyclopedia

A sleepover, also known as ~~a pajama party or a slumber~~ *the best kind of* party *(even if we are getting kind of old for them)*, is a party most commonly held by children *(see?)* or teenagers, where a guest or guests are invited to stay overnight at the home of a friend, sometimes to celebrate ~~birthdays or other special events~~ *Trisha passing her grade six piano exam like a total rockstar.*

Common Events

Typical participant activities include staying up late *(obviously)*, talking *(no, really?)*, eating *(Trisha's dad makes the best nachos)*, and playing until falling asleep *(as if we ever sleep)*. Common activities include playing board games or video games *(boring)*, having pillow fights *(yeah, right)*, and playing party games such as Truth or Dare? *which nobody ever admits to wanting to play, even though we used to do it all the time. I guess Truth or Dare's not cool anymore.*

Trisha's sleepover was yesterday, and now I'm so tired it feel like I've got million-ton barbells strapped to my eyelids. I did try to get some sleep, but, well, things got a bit weird.

Trisha fell asleep pretty early (she must have been pretty wiped from all her practising), but Chloe and Stacey stayed up almost all night, and so did I. And now my world's-heaviest eyelids won't stay open long enough to let me finish my homework for tomorrow morning. We were supposed to be charting the cycle of the moon for the last week, but I totally forgot to keep track. I think two nights ago it was a waxing gibbous, but that sounds more like some kind of monkey than a phase of the moon.

Waxing Gibbous

From Wikipedia, the free encyclopedia

Waxing Gibbous is the fifth studio album by Scottish singer-songwriter Malcolm Middleton, released on June 1, 2009 on Full Time Hobby.

Not even the faithful Wiki can help me today.

Anyway, the sleepover was a little weird, but it was still a lot of fun. I was especially glad to see Trisha's dad putting the final touches on a giant pile of his famous nachos as soon as I got in the front door. I charged downstairs to the basement and saw that Chloe and Stacey were already setting up their sleeping bags. I asked why we were laying our beds out so early when we were going to be hanging out in the basement all night.

"My back's been sore all week," Chloe said, making a face and massaging her lower back with both hands. "So I really need to sleep against a wall tonight."

"Yeah," said Stacey, "and I told Chloe that I'd sleep next to her because I know what to do if her back starts hurting in the middle of the night."

"So what do you do?" I asked, dumping my backpack and rolled-up sleeping bag on the couch.

"It's complicated," Chloe said, frowning, "but my mom does it for my dad all the time."

"Oh, okay," I said, picking up my sleeping bag again. "Then I guess I'll sleep next to you, Stace."

"Actually," Chloe said, "Trisha just called that spot."

"So I'm on the other end?" I said, trying to hide the disappointment in my voice.

"Yeah," Stacey said, looking apologetic, "I guess so."

Then Trisha came down from the kitchen, following her dad, carrying napkins to go with the giant nacho platter her dad was cradling in his oven-mitted hands. He put the tray down on the coffee table by the couch.

"Careful not to burn your tongues off, okay?" Trisha's dad said, taking off one of his oven mitts and wriggling his fingers at us. "This cheese is seriously molten."

Don't get me wrong, I loved that he'd made us this mega-snack, but did he think he was talking to kindergartners?

Still, the nachos were as delicious as always. I really did almost burn my tongue from all the hot, gooey cheese and homemade spicy salsa. The only one who didn't totally chow down was Chloe. And after a few minutes of stuffing our faces we finally noticed that she hadn't joined in.

"What wrong?" Stacey asked. "Are they too hot?"

"No," she said, "they're fine. I shouldn't say it."

"Say what?" I asked, mid-bite.

"Yeah," said Stacey, "what do you mean?"

"I just mean …"

She paused like she really didn't want to be the one to break some particularly gruesome news to us, but a bit like she was really enjoying herself, too.

"Do you guys know how much fat is in those?" she said finally, flicking at a particularly cheddary chip.

"So?" I said, my mouth still full of salty goodness.

"I'm just saying," said Chloe, "that I want to start being more careful about what I eat. I read this article about how we all eat way more sodium than our bodies know what to do with. It's basically killing us."

When did everyone start reading articles that told them what to do?

"Who cares?" I said. "We're kids."

"Maybe you are," Chloe said. She said it pretty quietly though, almost like I wasn't supposed to hear it.

Anyway, it was pretty strange hearing her talk like that. She's never seemed to care about healthy eating before — even when Stacey goes on and on talking about the calories in the juice we drink at lunch, which is totally annoying and definitely something she picked up from her sister Becca. As long as I've known her, Chloe's always bought cookies and chocolate bars at the corner store after school — she's even more of a junk-food addict than I am. So it was super weird to hear her suddenly spouting off about fat and salt. Okay, sure, I know that if I want to stop being the chubby kid in class I could stand to eat less junk food, but when there's a giant tray of nachos sitting in front of you that you've been looking forward to eating all week, those thoughts go pretty much right out the window.

But once Chloe got going listing off the horrors of saturated fat, Stacey stopped eating, and, instead of devouring all that gooey deliciousness in front of us, just sat there picking at the chips that didn't have cheese on them. Skinny little Trisha kept eating, though, and so did I. But the chips didn't taste quite as good after Chloe's big speech, and with the giant nachos split mostly between Trisha and me, we both ate way too much and afterwards I felt sick.

I spent the rest of the night feeling like I had a greasy cheese baby in my belly. I still had fun and everything, but it sort of felt like I was moving in slow motion, like I was out of sync with my friends.

Trisha lives just down the street from our school (I live close by too, I'm only a few blocks away from Trisha), so we decided to go for a walk and see if anything weird was going on in the schoolyard after dark. Well, we didn't all decide to, it was definitely Chloe's idea, but everybody else thought it sounded like fun. I didn't really want to go at first. My mom and I go for walks at night together sometimes — "Just pretend we're walking the dog," she says, even though she's allergic and would never let me have one — but she and my dad are pretty clear about not wanting me to go out alone at night. "You just never know who you'll run into," she says, even though we live in a really nice neighbourhood. But even Trisha was into the idea, and I didn't want to be the odd one out so I said okay.

I mean, really, we weren't even being all that sneaky about it. Trisha's parents knew we were going out (we promised we'd only stay out for half an hour and that we'd all stick together) and Trisha had her mom's cellphone with her with her — plus Stacey and Chloe had theirs — in case anything happened. So it's not like we were being particularly deviant, or maybe T's parents just didn't suspect that anything might be up. Still, I wondered what would happen if we came across a suburban drug deal or a late-night love connection. Fortunately, for the PG-ness of this story, we didn't. Chloe seemed pretty disappointed.

Still, it was kind of fun hanging around the schoolyard late at night. It was sort of spooky seeing a place we knew so well after dark. We chased each other around the

building to keep warm — it was still pretty cold outside
— and peered into the windows to see if we could spot
late-night janitors getting up to anything suspicious. Like
I said, we didn't find much. Chloe claimed she'd found a
condom, but she kicked it away so fast it could have just
been a balloon or even a stray Kleenex. Other than that,
all we saw were a couple of squashed cigarettes next to a
pile of dirty snow by the parking-lot doors.

"You don't think any of the teachers smoke, do you?"
I asked.

"Didn't you ever notice how bad Mr. Fischer's breath
smelled every time we came back inside from recess last
year?" Chloe asked. Mr. Fischer had been our teacher for
grade six. "He'd just sit in his car, chain-smoking and listening to jazz on the radio. He's been majorly depressed
ever since his wife left him for another woman."

"How'd you figure that out?" asked Trisha.

"I have my sources," said Chloe.

"Yeah," Stacey piped in, "he's so pathetic. He
smokes so much that he smells like my Aunt Louise,
and her teeth are practically brown."

"Gross," I said. "I'd never kiss a smoker."

"Ha!" Stacey said, "You wanted to make out with
Mr. Fischer?"

I said no really fast, but everybody laughed at me anyway. Even though I obviously hadn't meant it that way.

"No, of course not," Chloe said, making her face all
serious, trying to stop herself from giggling, "She wants
to do it with your Aunt Louise!"

The three of them laughed forever about that one.

I was embarrassed, but I was kind of mad, too. I didn't really think I'd said anything weird; it felt like Chloe had twisted my words around. I'd never been out of the loop with my friends like that before, the centre of the joke. I didn't like the feeling at all.

"Yeah, right," I said. "Stop it, guys, it's not funny."

But that just made them laugh harder.

"Don't be embarrassed, Jo," Chloe said between giggles. "I think you guys would make a great couple."

And they kept laughing, and maybe it was just my out-of-sync brain talking, but I really couldn't handle being a joke to my three best friends.

"I'm going home," I said.

"What, to your house?" Trisha said.

"Yeah, I'm leaving."

"Oh, come on," Stacey said, "don't be like that. It was just a joke."

"It wasn't funny."

"Yeah, it was," Chloe said. "It was hilarious. Your face got so red."

"It did not."

"Come on," Trisha said, "who cares? It's freezing, let's just go back to my house. You coming, Jo?"

I was still embarrassed, but I was more ashamed that I'd made such a big deal out of the joke. These girls were my best friends, my only friends, did I seriously think they were trying to be mean to me?

"Fine," I said. "It's no big deal."

We were all pretty quiet on the walk back to Trisha's house. It was getting late, and when we got in, her mom told us that it was probably time to get ready for bed. I took the little plastic jar of Oxy pads that my dad had picked up for me at the drugstore out of my overnight bag along with my toothbrush, and headed upstairs to the bathroom.

I'd had my hair down all day to cover up a giant zit on the back of my neck, but I put it up in a ponytail so I could clean my face. I took my glasses off and put them next to the sink, unscrewed the lid of the Oxy jar, and took out one of the little pads soaked in something that smelled a whole lot like toxic chemicals. It stung like crazy when I wiped the pad against my giant volcano of a zit, and I clenched my eyes tight and tried not to swear.

No one else I know has to deal with this, I thought. And as much as I know that it's not the end of the world, I hate having something that sets me apart as different. No, that's not really what I mean — all my friends are different, it wouldn't be any fun if we were all the same. I guess I just hate having to deal with this alone.

Just as I was finishing up, I felt an itch on the back of my neck. I reached up to scratch it and accidentally raked my nails over my enormous pimple instead. Then I really did swear. Pretty loudly. Trisha's mom stuck her head out of the bedroom door and gave me a look — though it was probably more of surprise than anything. She looked like I'd just popped a balloon in her face. I felt so guilty that I rushed back downstairs before I could say I was sorry.

Trisha passed out pretty much as soon as I got downstairs. Like I said, she must have been seriously wiped out. But Chloe and Stacey were lying in their sleeping bags, too, so I figured I'd get into mine.

"Aren't you guys going to brush your teeth?" I asked.

"No," Chloe said, "I forgot to bring my toothbrush."

"Yeah," said Stacey, "me, too."

They stayed up practically all night talking together, and their giggling kept me awake. I know I should have just dragged my sleeping bag over and joined in, but it kind of seemed like they didn't want me to. Chloe kept saying the names of other girls in our class, girls we're not friends with.

Chloe: Oh yeah, *mumble mumble mumble*, but Maylee said *mumble mumble*.

Stacey: Yeah? She *mumble*?

Chloe: *Mumble mumble*, and Janet.

Stacey: *Mumble mumble mumble?*

Chloe: *Mumble*, and Nadja, too.

I couldn't tell if my stomach hurt so badly from all that nacho cheese or just from being left out.

FIVE

Meeting

From Wikipedia, the free encyclopedia

In a meeting, two or more people come together to discuss one or more topics, often in a formal setting *like our living room, where none of the furniture matches and the carpet still smells like last year's science fair project (when I tried to teach my old hamster Mariette to run through a maze, and she escaped, leaving a trail of wood shavings behind her. That wasn't how she died, though. Dad eventually found her hiding behind the couch, and I wound up experimenting on a mouldy piece of bread instead. She died about a month after that and we never found out why.).*

In a family meeting — which is something we've never had to have before — Zim comes home with his girlfriend, Jen, and Mom and Dad sit down with them in the living room to have a serious talk that doesn't include me. Nobody has the bright idea to send me out of the house, though, so I can hear everything they say anyway.

Adults can be pretty short-sighted, even when they don't need glasses.

Ha ha ha.

Wow.
Wow.
Whoa.

This changes everything.

This huge, unbelievable thing that is so much bigger than all of my stupid little problems — the reason why Mom and Dad called the family meeting is (I still can't believe it — it's too weird, it's way too weird) J, Jen, is pregnant.

Z is going to be a dad.

Zim. My brother. The twenty-four-year-old record-store clerk. Roommate of Swirly/Kevin-Mike-Mark. Gatekeeper of the pepperoni/toxic waste dump.

Holy wow.

I went to bed early because I didn't know how to face Mom and Dad after their little meeting.

Were they going to try to act all normal around me?

Should I tell them that I'd heard what they said?

My nervous stomach gave me a definite answer to that question: N-O.

I lay face-down on my bed with a pillow under my stomach and another one under my head. I turned off all my lights so that they'd think I was sleeping.

Much later, after I'd heard Z leave and my mom and dad go to sleep (Mom poked her head in, but I fake-snored and she left me alone), I snuck out of my room and down the hall to the bathroom. I brushed my teeth and washed my face. I examined my pimply skin from a dozen different angles — my face only inches from the mirror — popping a few of the juicier zits on my cheeks and my forehead, and wiping the nastiness they left behind on the mirror away with a piece of toilet paper. I couldn't stop picking at my face. I knew it was late and that I was only making my skin more red by touching and squeezing every ugly bump, but I couldn't stop. My face and my fingers itched, and my stomach made loud, anxious noises.

When I was finally able to stop my hands, I smeared benzoyl peroxide cream all over my face. Dad had picked this tube of goo up at the pharmacy after I told him about the horrors of the Oxy pads — he said the pharmacist told him that this space-alien-sounding stuff is supposed to be the best thing for zits. So far all it seems to be good for is making my skin dry and flaky. When I was finished rubbing the stuff all over my face, I recapped the tube and washed my hands. I looked at myself in the mirror with my hands over my stomach, trying to keep calm the storm.

I thought about saying something to myself, standing there like the way people do in the movies. Something to calm myself down and make me feel better. Like a mantra or something. I didn't, though. I didn't want to wake my parents up.

Back in my room, I turned my iPod speakers on, low enough so Mom and Dad couldn't hear me. I scrolled through my music, finally choosing Bob Dylan's *Blonde on Blonde*, and tried my best to fall asleep. And not to think about J's belly.

Getting bigger. And bigger. And bigger. With a baby in it.

And that Z was going to have a kid.

And that I was going to be an aunt, I guess.

Weird.

Wow.

Whoa.

SIX

Sexual intercourse

From Wikipedia, the free encyclopedia

Sexual intercourse, also known as copulation or coitus *(ugh)*, commonly refers to the insertion of a male's penis into a female's vagina for the purposes of sexual pleasure or reproduction *giving your parents and your sister fifteen heart attacks each. Thanks, Zim.*

Sexual intercourse can play a strong role in human bonding — *yeah, and so can playing video games and going on bike rides and making cookies and watching movies and* not *making babies* often being used solely for pleasure and leading to stronger emotional bonds.

Sexual intercourse is apparently what Z and J have been having in his gross apartment in Parkdale.

Do they do it while Swirly/K-M-M is home?

No wonder Z never wants to invite me over.

My mom and I never had "the talk." You know, the whole facts-of-life/birds-and-the-bees squirm-fest? We never exactly got around to it.

Which was totally fine with me. Stacey told me how mushy her mom got the first time she got her period, and it sounded pretty embarrassing. Chloe got a book, Trisha and her mom looked at some website together.

I got nothing.

I was actually pretty glad that we'd skipped that whole step at the time, but now I'm not so sure. It seems wrong, kind of. I'm not sure how to explain it.

When I got my period for the first time — the morning after my eleventh birthday, like my body had some kind of switch that got flipped when I blew out the candles on my cake the night before — she still hadn't explained the whole deal to me. Not that she needed to; between the videos they showed us in health class at school, and stuff I'd seen on TV and the Internet, not to mention the fact that Stacey beat me to it, I wasn't exactly surprised when I bled for the first time.

I didn't even tell Mom for a while because I thought she wouldn't want to know. I kept hoping she'd ask me if it had happened so I wouldn't have to just tell her. Or maybe she'd get the hint from one of my friend's moms or something.

I managed okay with toilet paper in my underwear the first time it happened, but eventually I had to ask her to buy me some pads. She drove right out to the store and came home with a package filled with things the size of a Barbie inflatable raft (for fun in her dream house's pool, of course). When I finally used them all up I had to ask her to buy the thin ones, the ones Stacey has, that don't feel like you're wearing a diaper.

Anyway, my point is that my family doesn't talk about sex.

We don't.

So how are we supposed to deal with this?

Stacey just left.

I called her house first thing this morning — at seven-thirty, even though she hates getting up early on Saturday — after I woke up to a giant bleach stain on my pillow from that ghastly (old-school word, I know. But look it up, it fits perfectly) cream that Dad bought. I pretty much forced her to come over immediately. Not because of the stain, I mean. Because of the Holy-Wow thing.

It's a little after ten-thirty now.

At night.

I couldn't face my family without reinforcement today, and Stacey knows me better than anyone. Still, I guess it was kind of a long day for her to be running interference. I could tell she was starting to droop after dinner (we ordered pizza with black olives and sun-dried tomatoes, our favourite, and ate it in my room) when she started talking about how she should probably go home so she could get her schoolwork finished for Monday. She explained that she wasn't going to be able to do any work tomorrow because Becca just signed some major modelling contract and their whole family was going to go up to Collingwood for a ski trip to celebrate. Ski Slope Sunday definitely sounds better than Serious Family Discussion Sunday.

To take my mind off *the pregnancy*, Stacey offered to give me a makeover, something she's been dying to do ever since my face started seriously breaking out. She said it would help with my look.

What look — pimple princess? Somehow I don't think a makeover is going to get me runway-ready.

Stacey jokes around a lot about clothes and makeup like she doesn't care about them. She says that's Becca's thing. But she definitely knows how to turn it on when she wants to, that glamour/style thing that I have absolutely no sense of. I think I was born without that particular button.

To be completely honest, I think Stacey dresses kind of boring. I mean I know I don't look pretty or popular or even cute most of the time, but I think that dressing a little bit differently is sort of cool. I mean, not *cool* cool, but, I don't know … unique?

Z used to have lots of friends over to the house when he was in high school. I don't remember too much from back then, but I sometimes used to sneak down to the basement to spy on Z and his friends, teenagers who looked like giants. They were a totally different species — talking about bands and movies I'd never heard of, wearing bright, wild clothes, laughing hysterically at jokes I knew I'd never understand — and I was so afraid they'd catch me looking at them and think I was a creep.

But I wanted to look at them.

All I wanted to do was look at them.

I was fascinated. Maybe a little obsessed. Probably a creep.

They just all seemed to be perfectly themselves and not afraid of anything. And that's what I wanted to be.

When Z moved out for university, he left a lot of his old high-school stuff at home, like those *Saved by the Bell* tapes. I found his old T-shirts and baseball caps, and I started wearing them as soon as I was big enough, even though most of his shirts looked like dresses on me. They were mostly band T-shirts and some shirts with slogans on them. Jokes I didn't really get, though I pretended I understood.

I've never really gotten to know my brother that well, but I guess I've always sort of looked up to him. I know I should want to wear girly stuff and makeup and be more like Stacey and the rest of the girls at school, but mostly I just don't care. I used to wish I had a big sister to teach me all about this stuff, or wish that Mom cared more about stupid things like hair and clothes. I guess I do still wish for those things sometimes. Or maybe it's just that I know I'm supposed to want them. But most of the time I just don't care that much about being a girl. A girl like Stacey, anyway. But I sometimes wonder if there's something wrong with me for not caring about that stuff. For not bothering to make myself pretty if I want someone — read: *boys* — to like me.

Boys definitely like Stacey, there's no question. At least three guys in our class have crushes on her, but Stacey doesn't like any of them back. I don't get that. If I knew someone had a crush on me, I think I'd pretty much automatically like them back. As long as they weren't totally weird. Does that make me desperate or something? It's kind of hard to say since the whole thing is a non-issue. I am totally unlikeable. Or at least I am as long as my face keeps looking like the surface of Mars.

(Which it seriously does. I looked it up on wonderful Wiki: bright red, and covered in bumps and craters.)

But sometime between now and when I get old and die, I'll probably find someone who wants to kiss me. Or do whatever it is that people who like each other do together.

Not what Z and J did, though.

Ew.

I had my first serious crush last summer, on Declan Walsh. I met him at the overnight arts camp my parents made me go to. He was in the music group, he played guitar, and I was in creative writing. But apart from doing sessions where we worked on whatever our art was, everyone at camp had do other activities, too, like arts and crafts, and we had that session at the same time.

I remember when I first saw him across the table in the arts and crafts hut, fiddling with an orange guitar pick and looking totally bored. I'd heard him singing as I walked past the music hall earlier that afternoon

— I was heading back to my cabin to look for my lucky pen and strategically avoid having to write an acrostic poem for the millionth time. He was sitting near the open back door, away from the group, where I'm sure he thought no one else could hear him. His voice was beautiful and soft, and I walked up closer so I could see him. His left hand slid effortlessly up and down the fretboard of his guitar, forming chords that made his fingers look like spider legs that I could just barely see from where I stood. He was amazing. And, fortunately, too wrapped up in the music to notice me staring at him.

Seeing him in the craft hut, it was hard to believe he was real. I kept trying to work up the nerve to tell him how good he was while I sat there gluing pompoms onto popsicle sticks because I hadn't been paying attention to what the day's craft was actually supposed to be. The crafts counsellor gave both Declan and me disappointed looks at the end of the hour when it was clear that neither of us had made any effort to build a birdhouse, the assigned project. I thought maybe Declan would see what a(n accidental) rebel I was and start to notice me, but he got up and left without even looking my way.

I used to watch Declan from across the dining hall during meals, too. He was always really quiet, unlike the rest of his cabin, who pretty much never stopped yelling and singing and flinging their fish sticks around. I liked that about him; that he wasn't like everybody else. He seemed so mysterious, plus he was incredibly talented. He mostly wore band shirts, bands that had broken up before we were born. The Beatles and Pink Floyd and the Ramones. You could tell his shirts weren't really old, though. He must've bought them at a store in the mall. Hot Topic, probably. I guess not everyone's lucky enough to have hand-me-downs from a cool older brother.

Mom tried to take me shopping at Hot Topic once, right after it opened in the Eaton Centre last year. It was pretty weird, like someone had raided a thousand cool older brothers' closets and put all their stuff up for sale at the mall. Mom couldn't get over how much everything cost, and I couldn't get over how much older and cooler and not-with-their-mothers every other kid in the store looked, so we left without actually buying anything.

Later, when we stopped for lunch in the food court — Mom had a salad, while I had poutine — I just sat there shovelling fries into my mouth barely looking at Mom and wishing I was there with Z instead.

My cool older brother.

A cool older brother who's going to be a dad and whose life is about to change completely.

Can you still be cool if you're a dad?

As it turned out, Stacey's makeover was a pretty good distraction from all these awful daddy-brother thoughts. She put my hair up in Mom's old curlers, and used what makeup she could find — mostly cheap stuff that Uncle Tim had given me in our family's Secret Santa gift exchange two Christmases ago. I was ten then, did he really think I'd use that stuff? I'm pretty sure he picked it up at a dollar store and that he didn't remember which of his nieces I was because my dad's family is pretty big.

It took Stacey ten minutes just to wash my face (she says you have to be extra gentle with zits, as if she's ever had one) and put cover-up on before she even started on the rest of my face. I have to admit it, though, I looked pretty good when she finished. Normal, almost. But there is no way I could spend half an hour washing my face and doing my makeup every day. Maybe just for special occasions.

Stacey's mom came to pick her up a little while after dinner, and she and my mom talked while Stacey put her coat and boots on. Mom wrapped her arms around me from behind as she talked, hugging me to her, which she used to do all the time when I was little, but hasn't in forever. It was kind of embarrassing and I squirmed a whole bunch. She wouldn't let go, though.

"I hear you guys are going up to Collingwood tomorrow?" Mom asked. I'd told her about Becca's big contract when she called us down to the kitchen for dinner. But Stacey's mom looked confused.

"That's news to me," she said.

"Aren't you guys all going to celebrate?" I asked.

"Celebrate? Stacey, I thought you were having Chloe over to the house tomorrow," her mom said.

"Oh, yeah, right," Stacey said, "I forgot. Chloe's coming over." She looked guilty; her eyebrows were practically sitting on top of her head.

After that she waved goodbye and the two of them got into their car and drove off.

"What was that about, kiddo?" Mom asked, releasing me.

"I hate it when you call me that," I said. "It's fine. I was just confused. My stomach hurts. I'm going to go upstairs and lie down."

"Everything okay? Want me come up and rub your tummy? Or make you some tea?"

"No. It's fine. And can you please not call my stomach my 'tummy'? Like, ever again?"

"Okay, Sweets. But maybe when you're feeling a bit better we can sit down and talk?"

"Sure," I said. "I just need to be alone."

Up in my room, my stomach really did hurt, so I lay down. There's nothing crazy about Stacey and Chloe hanging out alone, but why would Stacey lie about it? I closed my eyes and tried to shut off my brain, but it didn't work.

Z rang the doorbell not long after that. I guess because he works nights at the record store he can only come and visit really late — it was almost eleven. He must have come by to talk to Mom and Dad again. From the scraping of chairs across the floor downstairs, I knew that they were talking in the kitchen. I faded in and out of light sleep for about an hour, and then I heard a faint knock on my bedroom door.

"Who is it?" I asked, my mouth slow with sleepiness.

"Zim," he said. "You awake?"

"Sure." I got out of bed, put on my slippers, and padded over to the door, opening it halfway. Zim looked the same as always — his hair was messy, and there was a stain on his shirt — but he looked different, too; he looked tired.

"Hey," he said, playing nervously with the hair on the back of his head.

"Hi."

I waited for him to tell me about the baby. About his impending parenthood and the end of his life as a cool older brother as he knew it.

We stood there for a minute, just looking at each other. I was in my pajamas, black-and-white-checked with little fortune cookies all over them, and all of a sudden Z looked so much older than he really was. Maybe it was just the light (one of the bulbs in the landing did burn out a couple of days ago).

"Zim?" I asked.

"Yeah?"

"Are you okay?"

"Yeah," he said. "I'm fine. How 'bout you?"

"Uh-huh," I said, "I'm okay."

"Middle school's not killing you?"

"It's all right. Not great."

"Yup," he said, "that sounds about right."

"Yeah?"

"Yeah." He paused and gave me a little sympathy smile. "Jo, I don't want to scare you or anything. I know Mom and Dad aren't wild about me telling you like this, but I think you need to know."

Here it comes, I thought.

"I'm moving back in," Z said.

I braced myself for the rest of the news.

When he saw I wasn't saying anything, Z kept talking. "I'm moving back in with you and Mom and

Dad. And Jen's coming with me. We're moving in."

He looked at me like it was my turn to talk.

"Oh," I said.

"That's it?"

"What?"

"I just thought you might be, I don't know, a bit more excited or something."

"Yeah," I said, "I am. I'm just, you know, tired."

"Oh, good," he said, "'cause Jen's really looking forward to it. She's crazy about you, you know."

"Oh."

I didn't want to ask him why they were moving home. I couldn't. He was supposed to tell me. He wasn't supposed to be keeping this giant secret from me. He was supposed to just tell me.

I remembered the day that Z moved out, only three years ago. Dad and Z had been fighting a lot, mostly because Z decided not to finish university — he'd dropped out in his third year to work full-time at the record store. Dad thought it was a pretty stupid idea. I think Mom thought so, too, but she was a lot quieter about thinking it. Dad and Z had been fighting about how he wasn't taking his life seriously, and how the record store wasn't a proper job. Z said that he loved working there — he'd been a part-timer since his last year of high school and they'd finally offered him a full-time spot. He said that it would be nuts to pass on an offer like that. But Dad didn't exactly agree.

Mom cried a little bit the day Swirly/K-M-M drove up to the house in his old beat-up van to help Z move his stuff to their new apartment. She cried, but I don't think she thought I could see her do it. And, I mean, it wasn't waterworks or anything. Just a little bit. A couple of tears.

But I knew that Z moving back in to the house, especially with J, was a bad, bad sign.

"Is everything okay?" Z asked, noticing whatever confused and sad look I had on my face.

He really wasn't going to tell me why they were moving. He was going to let Mom and Dad do the dirty work.

"Yup." I cleared my throat. "Fine."

"All right, cool. Uh, do you mind cleaning your stuff out of my old bedroom? Jen and I are gonna need it."

"Sure. Yeah. Right. I mean, okay. I'll clean it tomorrow."

"Thanks, bud. I owe you one." Z extended his hand for a high-five, and I slapped at it lamely.

"Night," I said.

"G'night."

I closed the door and listened to Z's footsteps as he walked back down the stairs, put on his shoes, zipped up his coat, and left.

Either Mom or Dad went down a few minutes later and put the deadbolt on the door.

I lay awake in bed for what felt like hours.

For the fact that the house was going to be bursting with people very, very soon, I'd never felt so totally alone before in my life.

SEVEN

Ginger (disambiguation)

From Wikipedia, the free encyclopedia

Ginger is a delicacy, medicine or cooking spice made from the stem of the plant *Zingiber officinale*. It may also refer to:

Ginger Baker (1939), rock drummer with Cream and Blind Faith

Ginger, the main character in the film *Chicken Run*

A word of British origin referring to people with red hair sometimes used in a derogatory sense.

A word someone scrawled with a giant red Sharpie on Chloe's locker before school this morning. A word that makes Chloe so mad she insists that we have to track down the culprit and make them pay for humiliating her. How exactly she expects three weakling girl geeks (well, two geeks and one model-in-disguise) to help her take down a permanent marker–wielding criminal is most definitely beyond me. But she says we need to back her up, that we're a gang, so we're going to meet at her house after school today to make a plan. Anything that lets me avoid going home is fine by me.

I faked sick all day Sunday so I could escape from talking about the whole Z/J situation with my parents. I guess they figure that Z's already told me. Still, it is kind of weird that they haven't made me talk about how I'm feeling. Faking a stomach ache never worked this well when I was little. Maybe Mom and Dad don't want to talk about it either. Still, if it's really happening, it's not like they have that much of a choice.

I couldn't stop thinking about it all day. I didn't even notice that anything was wrong with Chloe until we got let out for lunch. I guess I was kind of distracted. And that made Chloe mad, too, me being so spacey. She thought I wasn't taking it seriously. I was though, mostly. Maybe not that *seriously. It just really didn't seem like that big a deal compared to everything else that's going on right now. Yeah, it's embarrassing, but it's just a word, right?*

But it's important to Chloe, to the gang, so I'm going to focus:

Who would write Ginger *on Chloe's locker?*

And why is that word such an insult?

Chloe's house is sort of strange. For one thing, her parents don't buy any juice or pop, so Chloe always has to sneak some home after school. She drinks more sugar than anyone I know, but she keeps it totally secret from her parents. It's kind of weird.

Chloe sat us all down in the living room and made a big deal about how we all had to take off our shoes and be sure not to spill anything on the couches. I'm usually pretty careful, but Chloe's warning made me kind of paranoid. She didn't offer us any snacks anyway, so it's not like we had any food to spill. She had a big bottle of Coke that she bought at the plaza near our school after the final bell, but the rest of us didn't have anything.

"Okay," said Chloe, exhaling dramatically the way people never do in real life, "we need to figure out who did this."

Then Stacey started talking about who in our school she thought could have written it. I tried to pay attention to what she was saying, but everything sounded fuzzy. And, on top of everything else, my throat started feeling tight and itchy. Like maybe I was allergic to drama.

"Uh, can I have a glass of water?" I asked.

Chloe made a face. "The glasses are in the cupboard by the fridge."

"Thanks," I said, although I mostly just coughed.

To say that Chloe's kitchen is different from ours would be a bit of an understatement. I mean, sure, her living room looked like we'd stepped right into a catalogue, but I figured that at least the kitchen would look lived-in. Whenever my parents have people over they always wind up hanging out by the sink and the stove, even though there's never enough room for everybody. Dad calls it the heart of our house, our kitchen, and I sort of thought that's how it was for everybody.

But, like the living room and the rest of the house, as far as I could see, the kitchen was clean and cold and alien. There were no pictures stuck to the fridge with funny magnets, no overflowing bowls of fruit or even a single spoon or fork out of place. It made my throat even itchier. I opened the cupboard by the fridge to get a glass, but saw that they'd lined them up on a shelf just out of my reach — I guess Chloe gets her height from her parents. I almost went back to the living room to ask Stacey to help, but as soon as the idea occurred to me, I was embarrassed for thinking about it. It wasn't a big deal, I'd find a way to get it myself. No problem.

I went up on my tip-toes and reached for a glass. I was pretty sure I could grab one if I just hopped a tiny bit to nab it. So I bent my knees a little, fixed my eyes on my target and jumped, reaching my hand out for the glass sitting front-row centre. My hand connected, and I felt its cool slipperiness as I landed, but the second my feet touched the floor again I watched in slow-motion as it slipped out of my grasp, landed next to me on the stone-looking tiled floor and broke into a hundred tiny, glittery pieces.

"What are you doing?" Chloe yelled, coming up behind me only seconds later. She startled me and I took a big step backwards, landing, of course, on a big shard of broken glass. I yelped and grabbed my foot to get a look at it. The piece I'd stepped on was still stuck inside, and as soon as I saw it the pain became unbearable.

Stacey and Trisha raced in the kitchen after that, and Stacey helped Chloe clean up the debris, while

Trisha took my hand and made me sit on the floor away from the mess.

"How bad does it hurt?" she asked.

"Bad," I said.

"I'm gonna take it out, okay?"

"Okay," I said, squeezing my eyes shut.

"Ready? One, two —" And she yanked it out.

"Ow. What happened to three?"

"That's how my mom always does it," she said. "Three's too late." She surveyed my foot. "Oh, gross, you're getting blood all over your sock. Chloe, do you have any Band-Aids?"

"Bathroom," Chloe said, venom in her voice, "under the sink."

"Don't bleed to death while I'm gone," said Trisha.

"Yeah, right, thanks," I said, pulling my sock off and pressing a mangled tissue I fished out of my pocket against my wound.

Chloe and Stacey finished sweeping up the last bits of glass into the garbage.

"I think that's it," Stacey said, "I can't see any more."

"My mom's going to be so pissed," Chloe said.

"I'm sorry. It was an accident. I —"

"What, you couldn't reach?" snapped Chloe.

"Well … yeah."

"So stand on a chair." *You idiot.* She didn't actually say it, but her tone filled in the rest.

My face burned red. I looked at Stacey, silently begging for her to stand up for me. But she didn't say anything.

"Seriously, my mom is going to freak," Chloe said, rubbing her temples. Again, the way people never do in real life. "Those glasses cost like twenty bucks each. She loves them. She's going to be so pissed."

"I'm sorry," I said again. "I really am."

"Whatever, it's too late now."

"I could pay you back."

"They came in a set of four. What, do you have eighty dollars in your backpack?"

"No, but, like, I could —"

"Just forget it."

Then Trisha came back downstairs with the box of Band-Aids. And Chloe and Stacey went back to the living room without another word.

Trisha put the biggest Band-Aid in the box over the cut. I looked down at the bloodied sock I still held, bunched up in my fist. She was right, I had ruined it. There was a big splotch of blood where the glass had been stuck, plus it had torn a hole in the fabric.

"I think I better go home," I said. "Chloe's really mad."

"She'll be madder if you don't help with whatever revenge she's got planned."

"I don't know, you should have heard her just now."

"So buy her another glass."

"I don't think that'll work."

"Whatever, her mom probably won't even notice. You think anyone actually eats in this kitchen?"

"Yeah. I guess you're right."

"Come on," she said, slapping my arm, "you'll live."

I picked my sock off the floor and stuffed it in the pocket of my jeans. It bulged out — a big, embarrassing lump. I limped back to where my friends were gathered in the living room.

Chloe and Stacey were already well into making a list of everyone in our class who they thought might have written on Chloe's locker. We talked about the names they'd come up with for a little while, but none of them seemed very likely. So then, at Chloe's insistence, we made a list of everyone in our grade who could have done it. After twenty minutes of brainstorming and flipping through our old yearbook — which Chloe brought down from her bedroom — we still weren't any closer to sniffing out the red Sharpie vandal.

Nobody at school really likes our group (minus Stacey, of course), but nobody hates us, either. Or at least that's what I would have told you yesterday. Today I'm less sure.

It's hard to know what to say about Chloe's locker, because mostly I just don't care. It sucks, and she's right, it is completely humiliating to have the janitors called in to paint over your locker during lunch. But what are we going to do if we find the person who did it? They were probably just being stupid and trying to look cool to their friends.

Picking on a grade seven girl. Real cool, right?

But Chloe's taking it really personally, and she's making it such a big deal that it's kind of annoying. There are so many more fun things we could be doing, but instead we're acting all serious about some random jerk with a marker.

There are bigger problems. Much bigger.

After we finally exhausted ourselves with list-making, we had seventeen possible suspects: five in our class, eight in our grade, and four wild-card grade eights. None of them seemed any more likely than the others, though. We were stuck. Chloe kept saying that it had to be one of them, that we absolutely had to figure it out, but we had zero information to go on. What were we supposed to do?

A little while later, Chloe checked her phone and told us we had to get out because her parents would be home soon. Her house wasn't too far from mine and Trisha's so we figured we'd walk home. Stacey had to call her mom for a ride, though, and as Trisha and I put on our coats to leave, I wondered if that wasn't exactly the way Chloe wanted it, anyway. Me and Trisha. And Chloe and Stacey.

I tried to apologize for the glass one more time, but Chloe acted like she could barely hear me, running upstairs with Stacey before Trisha and I were barely out the door.

Me and Trisha.

And Chloe and Stacey.

My foot still hurt.

I wandered home in a sort of daze, I guess. I was surprised when I found myself at my front door without any real memory of having walked there, or of having parted ways with Trish.

And, as it turns out, I'd wandered right into a trap.

EIGHT

Ambush

From Wikipedia, the free encyclopedia

An ambush is a long-established military tactic, in which the aggressors (the ambushing force) take advantage of concealment and the element of surprise to attack an unsuspecting enemy from concealed positions, such as among dense underbrush or behind hilltops *or right in the front hallway of your house — like they were just standing there, waiting for you to come in — when you're hobbling home with only one sock on.*

Mom, Dad, Z, and J were all waiting for me when I got home.

"Sit down, kiddo," my dad said, "we've got a few things to talk about."

"Right now?" I asked. All I wanted to do was go upstairs to my room and listen to some music, or at least put on some clean socks.

J smiled at me. She waved. "Hey, Jo. How's it going?"

"Uh, fine." I was totally staring at her stomach — it was still pretty flat, you really couldn't tell — and had to force my eyes to move up to her face. J had shaved the back of her head completely, but had left bangs at the front. The hair she had left was a slightly faded pink. It was turning sort of grey, to be honest. "I like your hair," I added.

"Thanks," she said, rubbing her fuzzy head with her left hand and smiling like she really meant it.

"Sweetie," Mom said, "we, uh, well —"

"We've waited long enough to bring you up to speed," said my dad. "We were under the impression that your brother" — his eyes cut right to Z, squinting, and almost kind of mean-looking — "had explained what was going on to you."

"Sure," I said, "he did."

"Zim told you that he and Jen were going to be moving in, but he didn't mention why, did he?"

"No. But neither did you."

I was just telling the truth, but both Dad and Mom looked upset when I said it. Maybe because they knew that it was the truth, too. Maybe they were feeling kind of embarrassed that they'd left the job up to their son. I hoped they were. It all seemed pretty unreal that they thought they didn't have to tell me. They hadn't been acting like adults at all — they'd been acting like scared little kids.

"Look, Jo, I just know —" Z started. I could barely look at him; it was too, too weird.

"Who cares?" I said, my eyes fixed to the ground, "It's gross, I don't want to talk about it."

That was the truth, too. I took a tiny glance at J to see if she looked mad, or hurt, but her face was totally calm.

"I think maybe we should all sit down," J said.

"Good idea," said Mom, a little too quickly and a little too loudly, and she led us all into the living room.

Unlike Chloe's, our living room is tiny, like the rest of the house. We have a couch that fits two people and a big comfy chair next to it, but otherwise there's nowhere to sit, so we stood around for a minute, trying to figure out who would sit where. Mom wanted J to take the chair, but J thought Mom deserved it.

"Jen, really, you take the chair," said Mom finally.

"Okay," she said, "if you insist."

So J nestled into the chair, sitting with her feet up and bent underneath her, while Mom and Dad sat down on the couch, and Z and I picked spots on the floor. It was only when I crossed my legs that Mom noticed I only had one sock on.

"What happened to your foot, Jo?" she asked.

"Nothing," I said. "Just some broken glass, I stepped on some, I mean."

"Oh, you poor thing. Let me go get you a clean pair of socks."

And Mom was up and out of the room faster than I'd ever seen her move before.

"Does it hurt?" J asked, pointing to my foot.

"Oh, no. It's not a big deal," I said, staring at my foot to distract myself from J. "I was just being stupid."

"We've got to get you some steel-toed boots," she

said. "They've got tons of them at the Army Surplus store downtown."

"Yeah?" I said, thinking about how cool I would look in a pair of combat boots. Tough and cool, like J.

"Yeah, we'll have to go sometime. I've been meaning to pick up another pair, anyway. The soles are coming off on mine, so it kinda looks like they're talking to you when I walk." She held her hands up like puppets, flapping her fingers up and down to demonstrate. I couldn't help it, I started giggling.

Mom reappeared and handed me a pair of fuzzy pink socks, the ones I never wear.

"Here you go, babe. What's so funny?"

"Nothing," I said.

"Just a little invisible boot puppetry," J said, making her hands take a little bow.

Mom smiled, but it looked forced. Just her mouth smiled, not her eyes.

"I think it might be time to explain," Z said.

And then they all looked at each other like they expected someone else to do the talking.

"Jo, your brother —" Mom started, but then the words seemed to get stuck in her throat.

"I'm pregnant," J said.

My mom looked away. Dad sort of grimaced. Z reached over and put his hand on J's knee.

"Yeah," I said, before I realized what I was admitting, "I kinda knew that already."

Everyone froze. They looked like a perfect tableau of themselves. Stuck, like the instant after a bomb has landed, right before it explodes, ruining everything it touches. Mom looked terrified, Dad was confused, Z held a poker face, and J kept smiling.

"How'd you know?" Z asked.

"When you guys came over here before. When you first told Mom and Dad," I said. "I heard."

"You were listening?" Mom asked.

"It was kind of hard not to."

"Why didn't you say something?" Dad asked.

"I don't know. Why didn't you?"

This one was a second bomb, a smaller one, but I could see the blast in a wave that passed over everyone's faces. J was still the only one smiling.

"I didn't think it was right to confuse you like that," said my mom.

"I think we're all pretty confused," said J.

"Some more than others," Mom snapped.

"Whoa," Z said, "Mom. Not here, okay?"

We all turned to look at Mom, whose face had instantly flushed bright red.

"I'm sorry," she said in a small voice. "Jen, I apologize."

J had flinched a little at Mom's words, but didn't seem too fazed.

"It's fine," she said. "We're asking for a lot here, I know. It's hard for you guys, for all of us."

"It's no excuse," said Mom.

"Well, anyway," J said turning to me, "sorry about leaving you out of the loop, Jo. Or trying to, anyway."

"It wasn't right," Dad said.

"No," Z said, "it wasn't."

"Okay," I said, "sure. It's, uh, it's fine."

"We just wanted to wait until things were a bit more … decided," Mom said. "We wanted to have an idea of what our lives were going to look like, moving ahead, before we told you what was going on."

"You guys don't have to baby me," I paused. *Baby.* What a dumb word to choose. "You could have just told me."

"Yes, you're right," Dad said. "Anyway, we know that now."

"So Zim and Jen are going to have the baby and live in Zim's old room?" I asked. When I finally said the words out loud it sounded so ridiculous that I was almost embarrassed, though I couldn't tell if it was for me or for them.

"Not exactly," said Z. "We'll be staying there for now, though."

"We're going to have to get a bit creative once the baby's born," said my dad. "I'm going to renovate the basement so it's more of an apartment. So the two of them — well, three I guess — can have some privacy."

"And you're definitely going to have it?" I asked. "I mean, keep it?"

"Your mom and I have been helping these guys sort out their options."

"Yup," J said, "and this is our choice. We're going to have the baby together. Zim's going to be an amazing dad."

Z rubbed her leg and nodded.

"What about Jen's family?" I asked, afraid to even

look at her, afraid of how real this was all becoming. Surprised, though, that my mouth seemed to be asking questions without my brain's consent. All the stuff I'd been wondering about since I first heard, but had been too anxious to think about.

"I'm not really in touch with my family," she said.

"Oh. Sorry. Um, why not?"

"It's complicated," said Z.

"Sorry," I said again.

"Don't be," said J, giving me another warm, meaning-it smile.

"Are you guys going to get married?"

"We might," said Z.

"We may," said J.

"They should," Mom said.

"But it's their choice," said Dad.

"And if we do get hitched, you've got be my maid of honour, okay?"

"Sure," I said.

"With combat boots."

I giggled again, and Mom's tight expression loosened up just a bit.

"I think it's going to be great having you guys here," Dad said, though like Mom's forced smile I could tell he was trying to make himself mean it. "Zim, maybe I can finally teach you how to drive, huh?"

Z fought a frown. "Yeah, sure, you bet. It'll be great."

"Ha," said J, "we're going to be parents *and* drivers. Our friends won't know what to do with us."

"It'll be great," Z said again. And this time it sounded like he meant it.

"Why don't we all go out for some dinner?" Dad said. "You know, to celebrate."

But from the impact of this giant secret falling so abruptly off my shoulders — or maybe from my earlier blood loss — I felt completely exhausted.

"Um, I think I might just go to bed," I said.

"You okay, honey?" Mom asked.

"Yeah, I just want to stay here. You guys should go, though."

"I'll stay with you," said Mom.

"Okay," said Dad, "if you're sure. Zim, Jen and I can talk about plans for the basement. What do you guys feel like, burgers?"

"Jen's a vegetarian, Dad," said Z.

"Right, right, I forgot. How about Thai food?"

"That would be great," J said.

And the three of them got their coats and left.

NINE

Mother

From Wikipedia, the free encyclopedia

A mother (or mum/mom) is a woman who has raised a child, given birth to a child, and/or supplied the ovum that united with a sperm that grew into a child. Because of the complexities and differences of a mother's social, cultural, and religious definitions and roles, it is challenging to specify a universally acceptable definition for the term.

A mother messes up sometimes. But eventually she makes it up to you.

Mom asked me if I was hungry, and even though I wanted to be alone to think about what had just happened, my rumbly stomach answered for me. She nuked a tub of frozen mac and cheese for me and opened up a can of ginger ale. "For your stomach," she said.

She sat across the kitchen table from me while I ate, not saying much, but smiling in a far-away way. It was kind of annoying, but also sort of nice.

When I finished eating, Mom went upstairs to run me a bath. She even sat next to me on the bathroom floor once I got in. She hasn't done that since I was really little. I felt kind of weird about having her sit there while I was naked in the tub — even if she is my mom — but I didn't want her to leave either, so I didn't say anything about it. I think she was surprised I didn't try to chase her out. Part of me felt like I should punish her for the way she and Dad, and even Z, had kept the baby a secret, but a bigger part of me (a babyish part, I know) just wanted my mom to be my mom.

She looked calm, maybe a little shell-shocked. She hugged her knees to her chest and stared straight ahead, not looking at me as she spoke.

"I'm sorry we didn't tell you sooner," she said.

"It's okay." Which I didn't mean.

"No, it's not. It wasn't right to keep you in the dark like that. But I'm upset about this, and I didn't want you to be upset, too. It's okay for you to be feeling this way, any way. Any way you feel is normal, I want you to know that."

"Uh-huh." The bar of soap I'd been holding slipped out of my grasp, and I went searching for it through the bubbles. "Why are you upset?"

"Oh, lots of things. It doesn't matter. That baby is going to have a lot of love, that's the important thing." She turned to face me, and I sank lower into the water.

"But is there anything else bothering you, something at school?"

I nodded.

I told her most of what had happened with Chloe. About the locker and the twenty-dollar glass.

"That's pretty crummy about Chloe's locker. She was just upset, Jo, that must have been why she got mad about the glass."

"Yeah, I know, but it's not like I was the one who wrote on her locker. And breaking the glass was an accident."

"Why don't I call her mom and offer to buy a replacement? I'm sure we can find something nice at the mall."

"Okay," I said, grateful that at least one of my problems had a simple solution.

"You know, my girlfriends and I were always getting into fights when I was your age. I've always been impressed at how well you and your friends get along."

"Yeah. Up 'til now."

"Yes," she said, "maybe."

Then she got up and kissed the top of my head.

"If you want to talk any more about whatever's going on, I'm around."

I nodded again.

"And hey, maybe when we pick up a replacement glass for Chloe's mom, we can take you to get a haircut, too. There's a new place that just opened at Cloverfield, it looks pretty cool."

I knew that she was overcompensating for having kept the secret about Z and J for so long, and that she had no idea what cool was, but it still felt good. I wanted to resent her for it, but it was pretty nice having my mom back.

"I'm always here for you, kiddo. Okay?"

She was really laying it on thick.

"What about once the baby's here?" I asked.

She looked me in the eyes and squinted hard, not in a mean way like Dad's, just like she was concentrating.

"I will always be here for you."

TEN

Maturity (psychological)

From Wikipedia, the free encyclopedia

Maturity is a psychological term used to indicate how a person responds to the circumstances or environment in an appropriate manner, *like dealing with the issues of people twice my age and trying to stay sane — which is harder than it looks!* This response is generally learned rather than instinctive, and is not determined by one's age, *like how Chloe acts like she's so sophisticated, but then throws a tantrum like a kindergartner when I break one little glass.* Maturity also encompasses being aware of the correct time and place to behave and knowing when to act appropriately, according to the situation and the culture of the society one lives in *which no one I know ever is.*

At school the next day — Friday, thankfully — Chloe was acting super weird. She kept pulling Stacey aside to talk to her privately and was kind of ignoring Trisha and me. I asked if her mom had been upset about the glass I broke and she gave me a one-word answer: obviously.

I wanted to tell her that my mom and I were going to buy a replacement, but I thought maybe she needed the weekend to calm down. Like, maybe I could surprise her with a new glass on Monday and we could just go back to normal.

The two of them, Chloe and Stacey, went for a walk together at lunch and were gone for almost the whole hour. They were dressed almost exactly the same, too, which is pretty unusual. They were both wearing pink Hollister hoodies and skinny, light-blue jeans. It was a surprisingly warm day for February and neither of them wore a coat. From across the field, if you squinted, they looked like twins. I looked down at what I was wearing, black jeans and a baggy sweater and my giant winter coat, unzipped. I knew I didn't look anything like the two of them.

So while they were off walking, Trisha and I sat on the rusted-out jungle gym, knocking our salt-stained boots against each other and making up fake names for the band we decided we're going to start.

"How about Slush Puppies?" I said, eyeing the greyish puddle that had collected in the corner of the playground.

"That's terrible," she said.

So I hopped off and started kicking the pile of slush that had inspired me up at her. It splashed everywhere and got the legs of her cords wet.

"Ugh, see if I ever start a band with you now," Trisha said.

Then she jumped down and splashed me back until we were both soaked and giggling.

When we got back inside, our teacher, Ms. Vilaney, looked super annoyed at us for bringing all the icy sogginess inside. She sent us both to the washroom to clean ourselves up.

I heard Chloe whisper something to Stacey as we walked past them.

"Babies."

"Did you hear that?" I asked Trisha as I nudged the bathroom door open with my hip.

"Hear what?" she said.

"Never mind." I didn't want to snitch. Didn't want to spoil any chance I had of making up with Chloe by blabbing what I thought I'd heard to Trisha.

But the rest of the day was the same:

Me and Trisha.

And Stacey and Chloe.

ELEVEN

Hairdresser

From Wikipedia, the free encyclopedia

Hairdresser is a term referring to anyone whose occupation is to cut or style hair in order to change or maintain a person's image. This is achieved using a combination of hair colouring, haircutting, and hair-texturing techniques. Most hairdressers are professionally licensed as either a barber or a cosmetologist *or else humiliation machines from planet Mega-Hunk.*

How do I even begin?

How can I possibly explain exactly how wrong today went?

Okay, well, for starters, Mom and I went to the mall.

We went to the mall to buy a nice glass and to get my hair cut at that new salon she told me had just opened.

Only we weren't going to the real mall, the Eaton Centre, the giant one downtown.

Oh, no, we were going to Cloverfield.

Z used to make fun of Cloverfield all the time when he still lived at home. It's way out in the sub-urbs, where we live, and it doesn't have any brand-name stuff or even any cool alternative stores, just places trying to knock off what's popular. Z used to call it Cloven Feel, but I'm not sure why. I guess he thought it was funny.

The ride to the mall was actually pretty fun. Mom turned on the radio and sang along to some old songs she loved and I joined in when I knew the words. We're both terrible singers, but the sun had actually come out for once and I was feeling pretty good. I was going to take charge — of myself, if nothing else — and make the earth stop trying to spin ever so slightly out of orbit in a way that I knew was to blame for how things were starting to go wrong. Okay, so maybe my astronomy was a bit hazy, but we'd find the perfect glass, and I'd get a cool new haircut that — along with some killer combat boots — would show Stacey and Chloe how non-babyish I really was.

For starters, we checked out the discount house-wares store. There were giant bins of discounted Christmas decorations and creepy garden gnomes, and I got the definite feeling that we wouldn't be able to find a worthy replacement for Chloe's twenty-dollar glass.

"Mom," I said, pulling her away from the display of decorative throw pillows that had caught her atten-tion, "we're not going to find anything here. This stuff is way too cheap."

"This store has some really cute stuff," she said, grabbing one of the pillows shaped like a pair of big, cartoon lips. "Wouldn't this be fun for your room?"

"Mom, focus," I said, putting the hideous pillow back with its own kind. "We just need one glass, but it has to be good. Can't we go somewhere nicer?"

Mom stopped fiddling with another equally cheesy pillow shaped like a giant heart and looked at me seriously. "Sweets, with this baby on the way. We're — well, your dad and I are going to be helping Zim and Jen a lot, financially, while they're living with us. Zim's job just doesn't pay enough, and Jen's going to have to leave the bookstore once she has the baby. So we have to be a bit more careful with money."

I suddenly felt embarrassed for asking, but it's not like it was my fault we didn't have enough money to go around.

"Then why am I getting a fancy haircut?" I asked.

"Because you deserve one." She squeezed my shoulder.

I thought about snapping at her and saying something about how she was only taking me to get a haircut because she felt guilty about keeping me in the dark for so long about Z and J, but I swallowed the impulse. I was going to be a better person. Starting today.

"Anyway," Mom said, walking towards the aisle full of containers, glasses and bowls, "I'm sure we can find something nice here."

I followed her and we prowled the aisle together. Mom kept picking up one glass after another that was totally wrong.

"What about this one?" she said, pointing to a thin, blue-speckled glass.

"No, it was just plain glass. But with a ring of silver around the bottom."

"Like this?" she held up another one.

"No, that one's too tall. It was short."

"Like this?" Again, it was completely wrong.

"No, Mom," I said, starting to lose my zen-like patience, "that one has the silver on the top."

"Hmm, this is tough." Mom scanned up and down the shelf. "Do any of them look right, Jo?"

I shook my head.

When we'd gone up and down the aisle three times, I had to admit that none of the glasses was an exact match, or even close.

"I think it's the gesture that's important, sweetie." Mom held up the glass with the silver at the top for emphasis. "I'm sure Chloe's family will appreciate whatever we get."

I wasn't sure of that at all, but I figured a non-matching peace offering was better than nothing, so in the end we picked a set of two glasses that were the same basic shape as the one I dropped and took it over to the cash register.

The salon was right between the luggage store and the gourmet popcorn shop, where the off-brand sports jersey store used to be. This hip new Cloven Feel salon was called Dye, Dye, My Darling. Its sign was made to look like it'd been carved into granite that hung above the doors and a giant pair of scissors stood ready to take out any unsuspecting victims.

It was cool.

I was floored.

They were playing really loud music, I guess it was metal, but it mostly just sounded like we were walking through a wall of distortion and feedback as we entered, and I could see from my mom's face that it was already starting to give her a headache.

Correction: it was giving her one of her world-famous migraines that has to be treated immediately with tomato juice.

She handed me off to the woman at the front desk (who looked dangerously cool with bleach-blond hair, rings in both sides of her nose, and shaved-off eyebrows) and told me she had to go find some of her miracle drink, but that she'd be back soon to see how I was doing. .

The browless woman looked me over. "So," she said, totally deadpan, "what do you want?"

"You know ..." I started to speak, but her gaze was way too intense, so I stared down at my sneakers instead: Converse high-tops, black with mega-scuffed toes. "Shorter. Like —"

"It's fine," she interrupted. "We'll do something fun." The way she said *fun* was like a bullet flying straight out of her mouth. Direct and probably lethal.

"Oh, great," I croaked.

"Sure." She blinked a few times. I realized that when I'd lifted my eyes from the floor, I'd let them rest on the pale blank space above her eyes. I was totally staring.

"Take a seat," she said. "Marco will be with you in a minute. He's good."

I said okay, even though I'd never had a man cut my hair before. It made me even more nervous than I already was.

Chloe says that all men who cut hair are gay, it's one of her dozens of totally unproven theories. I don't think that's true, though. Or maybe it is, I don't know. Chloe thinks she knows everything about being gay because one of her cousins came out last year. Then again, she probably knows more than I do.

Anyway, ten minutes later, Mom still hadn't come back and a guy walked up to me where I was sitting and stuck out his hand to say hello.

Okay, he wasn't just *a* guy.

He was a completely gorgeous man.

He was this manly, amazing-smelling person, with perfectly ripped jeans and a plain white V-neck shirt with a little button stuck on the left side of his chest and a thick brown leather cuff around his right wrist. He was tall too, so much taller than me. He must have been over six feet, and he was perfectly skinny. A total rock star–looking guy, in the flesh.

"Hello," he said, as he reached out his hand, "I'm Marco."

And in that moment I was pretty sure I had died, I just couldn't figure out if I'd gone to heaven or hell. Sure, Marco was the most heavenly beautiful human man I had ever seen up close; that was undeniable. But seeing him standing there, smiling, with his hand stuck out and a pair of silver scissors barely peeking out of his pocket, I felt like the ugliest girl who'd ever crawled the earth. I could practically feel my pimples vibrating all over my face, underneath my hideous, greasy bangs. Even my zits were embarrassed to be seen next to this flawless specimen of a dude. I was red all over.

We shook hands (mine was completely clammy, ugh) and then he put his left hand on my shoulder, leading me over to his station. I was floating. Seriously. I couldn't feel my sneakers touching the linoleum floor. I'm pretty sure my shoulder had gone completely numb, too.

"Okay," he said as he sat me down in the big salon chair and checked out my hair. "So, what's the plan?"

"I don't know." I said. I squeaked, really.

"You want it short?" He cocked an eyebrow.

"Sure" I said, "whatever. Just make me look … ummm …"

"Cool?" He smiled and showed off a line of glistening teeth that would make a dentist weak in the knees.

"Yeah." I cleared my throat. "Um, I think so."

"Trust me, that won't be a problem."

I just nodded; I'd completely run out of words.

Marco brought me over to the sinks lined up against the back of the salon.

"Just relax," he said, pushing my shoulders down from where they'd migrated: just below my ears.

Oh sure, just relax while this male model runs his fingers through my nasty oily hair. No problem.

Marco wrapped a towel around my neck and turned on the faucet. He tested the temperature carefully, and when he was sure it wasn't too hot or too cold, he guided my head back into the sink and gingerly took off my glasses and set them aside. I sat there trying hard not to squirm as he pumped some shampoo from a big bottle on the counter into his hand and started massaging my scalp.

My legs — thighs — started tingling. I was terrified, trying so hard just to stay still.

"How does that feel?" he asked. His voice was rich and warm. It was chocolate, it was velvet.

"Fine," I peeped.

"All right," he cooed, "just let me know if it gets too hot."

"Sure." I couldn't manage to make a sound louder than a whisper.

When we were finished with the wash, he wrapped the towel around my hair and gave it a quick tousle.

"You're going to look great," he said. "Trust me."

Then we went back to his station and he went to work. He held his scissors like a jousting knight with a lance (or something equally manly and tough, I don't know, my brain was pretty shaken up at this point — it still kind of is).

I really hope that Chloe was wrong about men who cut hair. I just kept staring at myself in the mirror to try to stay calm — and to try to avoid staring at Marco. I breathed slowly and counted the pimples on my face while he worked.

When Marco had done most of the cut — it was so short I felt like I was practically bald, but I was too embarrassed to ask him to stop — he pulled out his electric razor from the drawer at his station.

"Okay if I buzz the back?" he sang, holding the razor like a microphone. "It'll look cool."

"Uh-huh." We'd already gone this far. I really was going to be walking out of the salon bald. How could I have let this happen?

"So," he said, as the razor nipped the back of my neck and I tried earnestly to blink myself invisible, "that's a great shirt you've got on."

I tried to remember what I'd picked out of the laundry hamper this morning. I was wearing a giant hairdressing bib over my clothes and I was surprised Marco had even noticed what I was wearing.

"Didn't I see a Nirvana shirt under that smock?" he asked.

"Oh, yeah." I cleared my throat. "Yeah. It was my brother's. They were his favourite band in high school."

"You like them?"

"Sure, they're okay."

"Yeah, what's your favourite album?"

Oh no. Oh no no no. Why did beautiful Marco have to ask me a skill-testing question about my T-shirt? As much as I love wearing Z's old shirts, I don't actually know a lot of the bands all that well. I mean, the Ramones, sure. "I Wanna Be Sedated" and all that, and Taking Back Sunday are great. But Dead Kennedys? The Cramps? To be totally and completely honest, I kind of just thought the shirts looked cool.

Does that make some kind of wannabe rocker loser?

Nirvana, I remembered, had a singer who killed himself, and they had a song called "Smells Like Teen Spirit."

But an album? I had a couple of their songs on my iPod, but that was it, I had no idea what albums they were from.

"Don't really have one," I said.

"Yeah," said Marco, "I like 'em all, too. You a Foo Fighters fan?"

"Uh-huh, yeah." The back of my neck was impossibly itchy, but I couldn't scratch it with my hands under the bib. "They're good."

"Yeah, I love Dave Grohl," Marco said, nodding. "That guy rocks."

"Who?" I asked.

"Dave Grohl?" He stopped buzzing. "Come on, you know Dave Grohl."

"Oh yeah, right." I coughed. "Dave Grohl. I think so."

"What," he said, "don't tell me you're a poser. You listen to the radio? You like 4EVR?" He said, naming a one-hit-wonder, C-list boy band that pretty well only kindergartners listen to.

He was joking. He was kidding around, I'm sure. But I sat there frozen, totally defenceless, just praying he would finish with my neck and I could get out of his chair.

"Come on," he said, "sing with me!" And he sang their only single to himself, perfectly off-key, "Baby, baby, baby, come to me, me, me. You're all I see, see, see, just you and me, me, me."

Turning to one of his fellow hairdressers, a girl with a bleach-blond pixie cut, Marco said, "This girl loves 4EVR! Why won't she dance with me?"

I was trying so hard not to cry that my face felt like it was going to explode. Marco just kept laughing and doing his little dance as he brushed the stray bits of hair off the back of my neck.

A million years of embarrassment later, he finally took off my bib.

I looked at myself in the mirror. The haircut was cool — J's style of cool, definitely not Stacey's — short in the back and shaggy in the front, but it made my goofy, pimply face looked totally out of place. I wanted to be cool enough to pull it off, but I knew that I wasn't, and I just felt awful.

Marco smiled at me in the reflection. "Great, right?"

"Uh-huh." I faked a smile. "Great."

Finally Mom showed up, with a can of tomato juice in one hand and the plastic bag with our discount glass set in the other.

"Wow," she said, gawking at my head, "it looks terrific, sweetie. Very funky."

I shivered. Funky wasn't at all what I wanted. Least of all coming from my mom.

Mom paid the girl at the front desk and then slipped five dollars into my hand.

"Go give your hairdresser a tip," she whispered in my ear.

"Please don't make me," I said as quietly as possible. My eyes were back down on my shoes.

"Okay," she said, rustling what was left of my hair, "whatever you say, sweets. He did a great job." She walked over to give it to Marco herself. Even she started blushing when Marco talked to her. He really was that beautiful.

I turned around fast to leave; I couldn't wait any longer to get out of the salon, this total monument of humiliation. But I turned around so fast that I didn't notice the guy who had just walked in until I literally smacked right into him, my right shoulder colliding with his chest. I jumped backwards and was about to blurt out an apology when I noticed who it was I'd slammed into.

Declan. Walsh.

No, no, no, no, no, no, no.

Declan Walsh, who I hadn't seen since the final campfire last summer. His parents had come early to pick him up that night, so I'd never had a chance to say goodbye (well, technically it would have been more like hello since we'd never actually spoken, but I'd spent all week psyching myself up to say something, anything).

And now he was right in front of me.

And even cuter than I remembered.

Which only made me feel worse.

And of all the dumb coincidences in the universe, that afternoon in the salon we were wearing identical Nirvana T-shirts.

Declan looked at me. He blinked. He said nothing.

My mouth had gone completely dry. I put my hands up to try to hide my freshly shorn head. "Sorry," I mumbled, willing myself to say anything else. But today my mouth wasn't working on behalf of my brain.

Declan looked at me. He blinked. He said nothing.

And I ran.

I ran out of the mall and through the parking lot until I found our car and collapsed on the hood. And then I started crying. That humiliating, hiccupping kind of crying where you can't get any words out and you're a total blubbering wreck, unfit to be seen by any human being except possibly your mother.

Mom found me like that, seventy thousand years later when she'd finally finished blushing at Marco. She wrapped her arms around me, rubbed one hand slowly up and down my back, whispering, "It's okay. It's okay. It's okay."

It wasn't, and it only made me cry harder, but it felt good just the same.

TWELVE

Friendship

From Wikipedia, the free encyclopedia

Friendship is a relationship and concern between individuals and provides positive emotional support. Friends care for one another and look out for each other *or sometimes they act really weird to each other for no good reason*. In order for a deep understanding to occur between friends it requires opening up about personal things, listening carefully, and being loyal to one another, *and not refusing to forgive someone for a dumb accident they tried really hard to make up for.*

I showed up early to school Monday morning, hoping I could talk to Chloe alone before first period and give her the glasses.

Mom and Dad both gave me a kiss before I left the house, which is sort of unusual for them. Not that they don't love me and want to wish me a good day and everything, but the house is always kind of hectic in the morning with Mom and Dad racing around to get themselves ready for work. Apparently they had all the time in the world this morning, though. Dad packed my lunch and Mom helped me fix my hair with some fancy styling gel she bought from Dye, Dye, My Darling while I was busy sobbing on the hood of our Honda. I had to admit, with it spiked up just right, I looked almost cool enough to pull it off. Or I would when it grew out a little. I'd been freaked out at how short it was at first, but it was going to be fine. I could totally rock it. Maybe.

I waited for Chloe by our lockers, but by the time the bell for first period rang she still hadn't shown up. Stacey was late, too, but that was pretty normal; she always complains that it's because Becca takes forever to get ready and her mom drives the two of them together since Becca's school is in the same neighbourhood as ours. So I put the glasses on the top shelf of my locker, away from the rest of the mess, and headed to class with Trisha.

"Cool hair," she said, as she grabbed her backpack and closed her locker. "We're going to have to take band photos soon."

"Yeah, definitely," I joked, secretly relieved that Trisha thought it looked good. "We're ready for the big time now."

We were more than a little surprised to see that Stacey and Chloe were already in class when we got there, sitting at the back of the class with a bunch of the popular girls. We took our usual seats at the front, and when the bell rang for lunch, I went back to talk to Stacey.

"Whoa," she said as I walked up to her. I'd already almost forgotten about my new haircut — class had been an almost-welcome distraction — and I self-consciously reached up to try to tousle my hair just the right way to make it match the almost-cool look I'd achieved briefly in the mirror that morning.

"Oh, yeah," I said, "what do you think?"

"It's, like, really short." Stacey sat back, appraising me. "But it's cute. It suits you."

"Yeah? Thanks. Hey, where were you guys this morning? I didn't see you at the lockers."

"Oh, yeah," she said. "Maylee told me that there were two spare ones by where hers is — you know, right by the gym? — and I figured that since it's such a pain to change clothes and everything after gym that it would be easier if I just used the locker there."

"Oh," I said. Huh? Did that even make sense?

"Yeah, and I told Chloe I was going to move, and she said it sounded like a good idea, so we both moved. Plus, I mean," she whispered, "Chloe's really wanted to switch lockers after, you know, *the thing*."

"Yeah, right." That did make sense.

By this point everyone had left the classroom apart from me and Stacey, and Trisha and Chloe, who were waiting for us. Even Vilaney had taken off for lunch.

"Lunch?" Trisha suggested, nodding her head toward the classroom door.

"You guys go," Chloe said. "I want to talk to Jo for a sec."

"We'll meet you guys in the lunch room," Trisha said.

"Actually, I'm going to go meet up with Maylee. She's helping me with my math homework," said Stacey.

"Yeah, I'll meet you by our lockers," said Chloe.

As Trisha and Stacey left, Chloe closed the door behind them.

"I'm glad you wanted to talk," I said. "My mom and I bought a couple of glasses to replace the one I broke the other day. I mean, I know they're not the same, but they're pretty nice. They're in my locker, let me just go grab them."

"This isn't about the glass," Chloe said.

"Then what?"

"I think you did it." Her face was deadly serious. It was freaking me out.

"Did what?" I said. I already knew the answer.

"The locker."

She didn't sound all that upset. She sounded like she had totally rationally solved the mystery and that she was one hundred and ten percent sure that I was the criminal mastermind behind the graffiti job. She almost sounded smug.

"What are you talking about? I'd never do something mean like that."

"Oh yeah? Just like you wouldn't get me in trouble with my parents by smashing their property."

"You know that isn't what happened."

"You're jealous," she said, "that Stacey and I have been spending so much time together. That we're best friends. It's pretty obvious."

"Stacey's still my —" I stopped myself. Did I really

believe that she was still my best friend?

"Just admit it."

We stood there for a second just looking at each other. I started to wonder if Chloe was going to hit me. She looked like she was seriously considering it. I wished I'd listened to Dad when he suggested I take karate last year. At least then I'd know what to do if Chloe's fist came flying at me.

But she didn't punch me.

She didn't do anything.

Eventually, I spoke. "You don't seriously think I'm the one who did it, do you?"

"Yeah," she said, "I seriously do."

Then she picked up her backpack from where it lay slumped on the floor next to her and left. As she turned to open the door, she said, "Oh yeah. And Stacey wanted me to tell you that she's not having a party for her birthday on Friday. She said she was going to tell you herself but she was afraid you'd cry about it. And by the way? No guy's ever going to like you with short hair."

And then she was gone.

Had that really just happened?

I stood there for a while, totally shocked into stillness. Thinking about Chloe, and the absence of her fist. About Stacey and the absence of her birthday party. About boys and haircuts.

Had that really just happened? It was too awful to even wrap my head around.

The world had crashed out of orbit and into the sun.

THIRTEEN

Ulen Township, Clay County, Minnesota

From Wikipedia, the free encyclopedia

Ulen Township is a township in Clay County, Minnesota, United States. The population was 163 in 2000.

Ulen Township has nothing to do with anything. Ulen Township is so tiny I bet I'm only the 164th person in the world who's ever heard of it. Today I clicked on the link marked Random article *on my favourite online encyclopedia because my head is spinning so fast that I can't think straight and don't know where to go, even online. Why is all of this happening now? And why is it all happening to me?*

I hope no one ever looks up Ulen Township again. I hope these words stay here untouched, forever.

But I know they won't. Someone a million miles away is already waiting to erase them. To erase me.

I wish I knew how to disappear for real.

I wanted to call Stacey this morning to talk to her about everything that was happening, how out of control it all felt, and what she was planning on doing for her birthday (her thirteenth!) if she wasn't going to have a party, but every time I picked up my phone, I couldn't make myself do it.

I thought about sending her a text instead, about trying to explain what I thought was going on with Chloe, but I didn't know what to say. Maybe I could just invite her to come over this weekend for a non-party birthday party? I didn't even know if that was okay. Did she just not want to see me?

So I called Trisha instead. Her mom picked up on the second ring.

"Hi," I said, "is Trisha there?"

"Is this Jo?"

Shoot, shoot, shoot. I hadn't spoken to her since the embarrassing zit/swearing episode at Trisha's sleepover. All of the sudden I remembered her face as I left the bathroom.

"Yeah. Hi, Mrs. Wynn." My voice was meek, innocent, terrified.

"Hi, Jo."

"Ummm." I buzzed, waiting for Mrs. Wynn to go get Trisha. But she stayed silent on the line, waiting for me to finish my sentence. I took a breath, praying for dumb courage. "I, uh, wanted to apologize for what happened at the sleepover. I'm sorry I swore in the bathroom. I don't usually talk like that. I was upset. I was, uh, having a problem."

"A problem?"

"A zit, actually."

"A zit." She sounded kind of amused.

"Yeah, it was really, um, painful, and — and anyway, it doesn't matter, I'm sorry."

"All right. It's not a big deal, but thank you for your apology. I used to have pretty bad acne when I was your age, too. It's no fun."

"You're telling me. But, um, can I talk to Trisha now?"

"Of course. I'll go get her."

I breathed out a giant sigh of relief, like cartoon characters do when they've narrowly avoided having a giant anvil dropped on their head from the top of a cliff. Then Trisha picked up the phone.

"Hello?"

"Hey, T."

"My mom said you apologized."

"Is that weird? I felt really bad about swearing at the sleepover."

"It's fine. But just keep a lid on it next time, okay?"

"I think I can manage that."

"So when's our first band practice?" Trisha asked.

"You mean Slush Puppies?"

"No, I mean the Flying Monkeys."

"Oh, too bad," I said. "I heard they broke up. The guitarist's in a new band, though. They're called Yeti Confetti."

"Oh yeah? Well my new favourite is playing a concert next week. They're called I Hate Mondays."

"Yeah, they're okay. I heard that Don't Touch My Squash is opening."

"Those guys know how to rock," Trisha said.

"They practically know how to boulder."

Trisha snorted.

"So can I come over?" I asked.

"Yeah," she said, "obviously. Bring Zim's guitar."

"Aye-aye, captain."

It's funny that Trisha and I don't hang out more often, especially since we live so close to each other. I walked over to her house, and we spent most of the afternoon talking and listening to music in her room.

Trisha's bedroom is kind of plain — still sort of babyish and pink, she hasn't changed it around too much since she was little — except for a few posters she's put up in the last couple of months. She's been getting really into this band she heard about called Mainline, and she ordered one of their posters online. It looks kind of funny in her room compared to the rest of her decor, but it's just another way that Trisha's very quietly doing her own thing. Lately she's been wearing weird tights to school, too — striped ones, or ones with cool designs on them. She changes into them in the bathroom, which is kind of weird because I'm sure her parents wouldn't care. I think she just likes the idea of having a secret identity, like a superhero.

She put on the new Mainline album for me, playing it quietly enough that her parents couldn't hear it downstairs.

"How did you hear about these guys?" I asked.

"I found their Facebook page and checked out some of their music. They're actually from around here, you know? They all grew up in Brampton, like an hour outside the city."

"Oh wow, you think they ever play here? I mean, in Toronto, downtown?"

"Yup," she said, drumming along to the music on her desk. "Their shows are always nineteen-plus, though. It sucks."

"Oh, man."

"I know. I'm never going to get to see them play live."

"I guess not."

We sat for a while, just listening to the record. The guitars were great, they wailed, but it wasn't like the harsh distorted music they were playing at Dye, Dye. This was kind of, I don't know, weirdly melodic? But tough; the singer was practically growling through the lyrics. She definitely wore combat boots.

"This is great," I said.

"Yeah, I know" said Trisha, as she turned the volume up just a tiny bit. She smiled, and she looked like she was drinking in the music right through her skin. Trisha's happiest when she's listening to music, I could just tell. No wonder she plays the piano so well.

We got to the end of the album without saying much else, and then Trisha started playing it again from the beginning. I held Z's guitar in my hands and pretended to play along, but it was tough since I didn't actually know any chords.

"Hey, Trisha?" I said, when we were well into the third song for a second time around.

"Yeah?"

"Do you think it's weird that Stacey cancelled her birthday party?"

"I don't know. She told me her parents were going out of town so she couldn't have us over. Something about how Becca had a modelling job in Montreal so they had to take her there for the weekend."

"Oh. Chloe didn't mention that."

"Chloe told you the party was off?"

"Yeah. She said Stacey was afraid I was going to cry about it or something. She's been acting super weird lately."

"Who, Chloe or Stacey?"

"Both of them. But I was talking about Chloe."

"Uh-huh," Trisha said. "Weird like how?"

"She thinks I'm the one who wrote on her locker."

Trisha paused and looked at me hard. "You didn't, right?"

"Of course not. You think I'd do that?"

"No," she said. "Just checking."

"I'd never do something to hurt her."

"I guess she was pretty pissed about that glass." Trisha got up to change the music on her computer.

"That's what I don't get," I said, turning on the bed to face where Trisha was standing. "All this over one stupid glass of water? Isn't that totally insane?"

"Yeah." Trisha nodded. "Anyway, I'm sure Chloe will get over the whole locker thing. Maybe you should just tell her you did it?"

"But I didn't, and she's the one who's acting totally weird."

"I don't know, Jo, you've been acting kind of weird the last couple of weeks, too. Spaced out, you know?" She found what she was looking for and put it on. Whatever the band was they were a lot more chilled out.

"So what?"

"I'm just saying." She flopped down on the bed again. "If you and Chloe are in a fight, I'm not picking sides."

"I'm not asking you to. There's — there's a lot going on right now."

"Like what?" Trisha asked.

"You know Zim's girlfriend?"

"Yeah, I remember you talking about her. You said she had green hair or something. What's her name, Jess? She sounded cool."

"Jen. She is. Her hair's not green anymore, though, that was months ago."

"What colour is it now?"

A trumpet joined in on the song. It sounded really good.

"Pink, but that's not the point. The point is she's pregnant. Zim's going to be … he's gonna be a dad, and the two of them are moving back home."

"Whoa," she said.

"Yeah," I said, "I know."

I told Trisha about everything that had happened. It felt good to tell someone how I was feeling, even if it wasn't Stacey.

Trisha mostly just sat still and nodded, occasionally making a sympathetic face, as I described the family meeting and everything my parents had told me about what was going to happen next.

"What does Jen mean, she doesn't talk to her family?" she asked when I had finished. "Like, at all? How is that possible?"

"I don't know. Zim says it's complicated."

"I believe that."

"I know. Man, I am going to be the most pizza-faced aunt who ever lived."

"Why do you always talk about your face like that?" Trisha asked. "It's not that bad."

"Are you kidding? Do you know how many different kinds of creams and washes and oils and cover-ups I have to use to even look half-human? My skin is disgusting."

"I'm just saying, it could be worse."

"I guess," I said. "It's just pretty hard to imagine."

"Don't worry. Everyone loves a girl in a band."

"I can't believe you found an upside."

"What can I say?" Trisha said, totally deadpan, "I'm an optimist."

Trisha didn't invite me to stay for dinner, so I walked back home around six.

Z and J were there when I arrived, with their first load of stuff for the big move. Dad was helping Z carry a futon frame up the stairs, and J was hauling a giant duffel bag toward the house.

"Do you want some help or something?" I asked.

"Hey, Jo!" She beamed at me. "Nah, don't sweat it, I've got this."

I wasn't sure if pregnant women were supposed to lift heavy bags. I couldn't remember if they'd said anything about it in health class. My mom certainly hadn't been warned against it, though. She wasn't anywhere around to help.

I found her later, upstairs reading a book.

"So. They're really moving in," I said, plunking myself down on my parents' enormous king-size bed next to where she lay.

"They really are," she said, putting her book down next to her and putting her reading glasses on top of her head.

"What are you reading?" I turned my head around to read the cover. It was an old book I recognized, one that had been on the old shelves in the basement forever. *The Wind in the Willows*.

"I used to read it to your brother when he was little."

"Oh. How come you never read it to me?"

"Your brother had me read it to him so many times that by the time you came along, I didn't want to hear about Mr. Toad of Toad Hall ever again."

"And now?"

"I may have some love for these silly animals left in me after all."

"Are you going to read it to the baby?"

"Yes," she said tousling my short, short hair, "I think I might."

FOURTEEN

Dermatology

From Wikipedia, the free encyclopedia

Dermatology is the branch of medicine dealing with the skin and its diseases. A dermatologist takes care of diseases, in the widest sense, and some cosmetic problems of the skin, scalp, hair, and nails *and acne.*

I guess it's official. I have clinically awful skin.

Mom made an appointment with a dermatologist in the east end of the city, Dr. Mueller, and picked me up at school today to take me to my first appointment.

Dr. Mueller's kind of cold — he didn't smile once the whole time we were there. He told me my acne was "unusually complex for someone of my age." Gee, thanks. He wrote me out a prescription for some super strong zit-banishing cream and told me to come back and see him in a month.

Oh boy, I can't wait.

If I thought the cream that Dad brought home from the drugstore had bleached my pillowcase, it's nothing compared to the awesome power of my new prescription-grade zit-zapper. Mom tried really hard to put on a patient smile when I wiped my face on one of her navy blue towels and left behind a pinkish-white smear, but I figured she was kind of upset that my face had spoiled her nice towels.

But seriously, if this stuff can strip the dye from a towel, is it really safe to be smearing it all over my face? What's going to happen if I get it in my eyes?

I don't want to think about it anymore.

My skin's so dry from this new cream that it's getting all nasty and flaky. But I can't put moisturizer on my face because that'll just block my pores — so says Dr. Mueller.

Acne is exhausting.

I should just let my greasy face be free. I almost wish I had the confidence to do that. To not try to cover up every single new spot I find, and to be proud to be the weirdo I am.

I wish.

Almost.

Z and J have now officially moved into the house, and J's belly is starting to show, just a tiny little bit, that she has a tiny little fetus or whatever inside of her.

Great Things about Having My Cool Older
Brother and His Cool Pregnant Girlfriend
Staying in Our House:

1. I almost, almost, almost feel cool by
   association when Z and J talk about a place
   they've been to or a band they've seen play
   and they tell me I'd like them.

2. Z says he's going to teach me how to play
   guitar sometime soon, which

   a) will be an amazing distraction and

   b) will make my band with Trisha an actually
   possible possibility.

3. J had to stop dyeing her hair because
   apparently it's bad for the baby, so she's
   planning on shaving all her hair off soon and
   she says I can wield the clippers if I want to.

Less Than Great Things about Having My Cool
Older Brother and His Cool Pregnant Girlfriend
Staying In Our House:

1. Five people, one bathroom. Well, if you don't
   count the one in the basement, which I don't.
   Spider central. Eek.

2. Dad's been bugging Z to find a better job,
   and it's completely irritating hearing them
   fight about it. Z's been working at the same
   record store forever and he says that the staff
   are like a giant family. Dad says he needs to

a) take parenthood seriously and maybe go back to school so he can make more money or

b) at least get a job that will give him (and J and the baby) health benefits.

3. Did I mention that we only have one non-spider-filled bathroom?

School hasn't gotten much better. Stacey still acts like everything's normal, but she never wants to hang out anymore. I found out that she spent her birthday with Chloe. They went shopping at the Eaton Centre and picked out more matching clothes at Hollister. For dinner they went to the Hard Rock Cafe, across the street from the mall. It was just the two of them, not even Stacey's parents or Becca were there. I heard Chloe tell another girl in our class, Maylee, all about it.

It's great spending more time with Trisha and everything, but sometimes she invites one of her friends from her church over instead of me so I have to find something else to do. It's not that they're not nice or anything — I could hang out with them if I really wanted to — they're just kind of boring. And they make me really miss Stacey.

I'm not going to tell Chloe it was me who wrote on her locker; I totally refuse to give in to her paranoia. I'm still mad that she accused me in the first place. These days she and Stacey do everything together. They link arms in the hallway and walk to class and lunch together. They're both so tall that it's like a human fence roaming the school. Nobody can get past them.

I'm pretty sure they like it that way.

One thing I thought was going to be a pro about Z living at home again is that my dad is teaching him how to drive. Z's had his learner's permit since he was sixteen, but he never actually learned how to drive. He used to say that he didn't drive for political reasons. Or, environmental, I guess. That the world didn't need the pollution of one more car — he swore that he'd ride a bike or take public transit everywhere, his whole life.

I guess his whole life was a bit shorter than he thought it might be.

At dinner one night about a week after Z and J moved in, my dad brought it up at dinner.

We were just clearing the table — J had made dinner, spaghetti with veggie meatballs and garlic bread, yum — when Dad slapped Z lightly on the arm.

"Let's go for a drive," he said.

"That's a great idea," J called from the kitchen.

"Yeah, it's about time you started learning," Mom said, as she helped me clear the table.

"Can I come?" I asked. I was dying to see Z behind the wheel. I imagined him putting some really great music on the radio and pretending he was driving me around like an impossibly cool chauffeur.

"Sure," Dad said, "it'll be good to practise with another passenger. Think you could pretend to be a crying baby, Jo?"

I made a face — what a bad joke.

"Why not?" said Z. "Let me grab my wallet. I'll meet you guys by the car."

Dad and I got our coats and he went searching for the car keys.

I listened to Mom and J talking in the kitchen.

"Dinner was delicious, Jen, thanks for making it."

"Happy to help. What did you think of the veggie meatballs?"

"They were ... interesting. What was in them exactly?"

"Let's see ..." she counted off the ingredients on her fingers, "eggs, bread crumbs, cheese, soup mix ..."

"Really?"

"Yup. Onion soup."

"Huh. Who'd have thought? Anyway, don't worry about cleaning up," Mom said, taking a dish towel from J's hands. "You cooked, you should have to clean, too."

"Naw, I don't mind," J said, taking the towel back. "I'll be fat and useless soon enough. Might as well help while I can."

"That's very sweet. I'll wash if you want to dry. Do you mind passing me that dishcloth?"

Dad came up behind me then, jingling the keys in my ear. I jumped about a foot and half into the air.

"You scared me," I said when he started laughing.

"Didn't you learn anything about eavesdropping the last time?"

"Yeah, that it's the only way to get any information around here."

"Touché, kiddo. But we're working on it, right? We're all one big work in progress."

"Whatever," I said. "Let's drive."

Sitting in the backseat with Z behind the wheel wasn't exactly how I'd pictured it. Dad wouldn't let him put the radio on their first time out, and he spent the first twenty minutes just walking him through the different parts of the car.

"Dad, I know where the parking brake is," Z said, pointing to a lever that stuck out the right side of the steering wheel.

Dad chuckled.

"I don't get it," I said. "What's so funny?"

"That's the turn signal, Jo. A little driving joke."

"Oh."

"You pay enough attention and I won't have to explain all of this again in four years."

"Three," I said. "My birthday's coming up."

"You're having another one?" Dad said. "And here I thought that they'd gone out of style."

"Ha ha," I said. "Shouldn't you two be talking about the car?"

So Dad finished explaining the basics to Z, and then we were out on the road. Small roads, of course; we just drove around the neighbourhood, but Z wasn't too bad. Of course there were a few tense moments — a stop sign that Z didn't see, and a couple of times Dad noticed him driving over the speed limit.

"I was only over by ten K," Z said of the speeding. "I've seen you do that around here lots of times."

"But I'm not the new driver."

"But isn't the law the law?"

"Don't get smart, just drive the car. The speed limit is *fifty*."

But we made it home in one piece. And I think Z actually liked driving. When we got home, he paced around the car.

"How much would something like this cost?" he asked Dad.

"We'll talk about that once you pass your road test."

"What do you think, Jo? I'm a pretty great driver, right?"

"Oh, sure," I said, "when you remember to stop at the big red sign marked STOP."

"Oh, is that what that means? Watch it. You better be nice or I'll never drive you to school."

"My school's only four blocks away."

"But think of how cool you'll look pulling up in the back seat of your brother's shiny red convertible."

"Wow. I'm pretty sure they'll crown me prom queen for that."

"Or king if you keep cutting your hair so short."

I put both of my hands up to my head. "I do not look like a boy," I said.

"I was just kidding, Jo. It looks great. You're so punk."

"Thanks," I said, knowing he was joking, but hoping there was some grain of truth to what he said.

And for a moment it felt kind of perfect. It was like my cool older brother Z had never left. We really were a family.

So the driving wasn't a complete pro, but it wasn't a con either. It was just all of us trying our best.

I slept well that night for the first time in a while.

FIFTEEN

Stacy

**From Wikipedia, the free encyclopedia
(redirected from Stacey)**

Stacy or Stacey may refer to:

Places

- Stacy, Virginia, a village *that is probably slightly larger than Ulen Township*

People

- Warren Stacey, British R&B singer-songwriter
- *Stacey Van Allsburg, would-be model and full-time Austenite, former best friend and confidante (missing her, missing her, missing her), seemingly stolen by the Linebacker, a.k.a. GINGER, aka Chloe Somerville, FF (former friend)*

Other Uses

- *Stacy* (film), a Japanese zombie horror film *(I looked this one up — it's about teenage girls who turn into zombies, I can totally relate).*

I just got back from my second appointment with Dr. Mueller. I really wish I could call Stacey and talk to her about this. It's freaking me out, but I don't think I can talk to Trisha about it.

Dr. Mueller put me on birth control pills.

Me.

On the Pill.

What the *what*?

He said it would help my skin, that the pill would keep my hormones under control or something.

What hormones?

Is this safe?

It's not like I'm ever going to be having sex.

I want to call Stacey so badly, but I can't. I bet she'd know what to say. I bet Becca's on the Pill, so she might know something about the side effects. Dr. Mueller said there would be side effects, but he didn't exactly get into specifics. He told me not to worry about it, and I was too embarrassed to ask him what it all meant. Dad was in the room with me — Dr. Mueller had to go out into the waiting room and call him in because I guess he needed parental consent to prescribe it. Dad tried to play it cool, but his eyes practically bugged out of his sockets when Dr. Mueller told us. What did these two grown men know about me and my body, anyway? Why couldn't Mom have taken me to the appointment?

I crossed my arms tight across my chest and stared down at my slushy boots. I wanted to melt into a puddle on the ground with the slowly dripping snow — to be mopped up and flushed away.

In the car it was pretty obvious that Dad didn't know what to say. He kept starting sentences without finishing them, leaving them to float up into nothingness like helium balloons when you let go of the string.

"Now, honey, it's not like …"

"You don't need to be thinking of …"

"It's perfectly normal to …"

I wanted more than anything for him to just stop talking, but he kept trying to put his words together — and kept letting go of the string.

We finally got to the pharmacy, and I handed over the prescription Dr. Mueller had written for me. When it was ready, the pharmacist handed me a paper bag and asked "Have you ever taken birth control pills before?" Loud enough that I'm sure half the store could hear her.

"No," I whispered.

"Okay. You're going to have to remember to take them at the same time every day, okay? Every day, no skipping."

"Sure," I said, nabbing the bag off the counter and bolting for the front door. I didn't even look back to see if Dad had followed me, though of course he had.

This can't be normal.

Dad told Mom about my prescription. I heard them talking about it in the living room. Mom sounded surprised, but it wasn't like she sounded worried or weirded out or anything. For someone who didn't even want to talk to me about sex, how is she okay with me being on *the Pill*?

I wanted to shut off my body, my brain. I knew I

couldn't, though. So I did the next best thing. I went downstairs to watch TV by myself in the basement.

The basement's a total wreck since Dad started trying to renovate it. I don't think he has a clue what he's doing, but he's trying hard to make the place more like home for Z and J.

I'd tried calling Trisha, but her mom said she was in the middle of practising piano. I could hear her playing endless scales in the background, so I said never mind, I'd talk to her tomorrow at school.

I sat there on a stray milk crate amidst the construction site, flipping channels for an hour without finding anything that seemed worth watching.

Later, Dad came downstairs to see how I was doing.

"Everything okay down here, kiddo?" he asked.

"Fine," I said, not taking my eyes off of the TV as the pictures flashed in quick succession.

"Anything you want to talk about?"

"Not really."

"Like what I've done with the place so far?" he asked, turning to survey his work.

"It's fine."

"Well, all right. Don't stay up too late."

"I won't."

Flip, flip, flip.

Nothing.

Even later, just as I was starting to get ready for bed, J came by my room to talk. It's pretty hard to keep a secret in a house this small. Z must have heard Mom and Dad talking about the Pill, and then told her about it. It felt

115

pretty awful to think that everybody knew about my new prescription before I even had a chance to figure out what it really meant, but I was still glad to see J's face at my door.

"Hey," she said, poking her head in, "can I come in?"

"Sure. Uh, how are you feeling?"

"Pretty good," she said, sitting down on my bed. "The morning sickness is getting a bit better. I can't seem to stop drinking apricot nectar, though. I'm, like, addicted."

"Yeah," I said, sitting down beside her, "the stuff Mom brings home from the health store near her work is good."

"I know, it's heaven."

"Mm-hmm."

"So, hey," J said, "I know it's none of my business, and you can tell me to butt out anytime, but I heard about your appointment today."

"Yeah. It's … um … it's kind of —"

"What, embarrassing?"

"They put me on the Pill," I whispered.

"Yeah, that's what I heard." She put her hand on my shoulder. "I was on birth control when I was younger, too, you know. Not that much older than you, actually."

"How old?"

"I think I was about fourteen?"

"I'm almost thirteen."

"I know." She took her hand away. "Next month, right?"

"Uh-huh. April seventeenth."

"Cool, I'm sure we're going to have an awesome party for you."

"Maybe."

"I'm sure we will. But anyway, about the Pill? Just watch yourself when you start taking it. Pay attention to how it makes you feel, okay?"

"What do you mean?"

"It's just … well, when I started taking the pill it really messed with my moods. I was depressed, Jo. Pretty badly, actually. But no one had told me that the Pill would do that, so I thought it was just me. Did your doctor tell you anything like that?"

"No," I said, trying to remember Dr. Mueller's exact words. It was all a mush-mouth blur.

"I don't want to scare you," she said, "and you're probably on a really low dosage anyway, but it's something you should know about. I wish someone had told me; I thought I was going crazy."

"So the Pill made you crazy?"

"Ha, no, I wish it were that simple. There's, uh, a whole lot of mental illness in my family. I guess I'm just more, you know, susceptible to depression because of that. I've got to be pretty careful. Take good care of myself, you know?"

"Oh," I said, "wow." Had J just admitted she was actually crazy? She was so calm and matter-of-fact about it, like it was normal. Wow.

"Sorry, Jo, am I freaking you out? I know I can go a bit overboard sometimes. I just wish someone had cared enough to tell me the truth about my body from the beginning, you know?"

"No, no, I get it. I think."

"Cool. I'm sure the Pill will be fine for you. But you can ask me anything if you ever start feeling weird, okay? Even if you don't."

"Anything?"

"Anything."

"Why'd you get pregnant?" I asked, completely without thinking. I clamped my hand over my mouth and slowly shook my head. What a dumb thing to say.

"I didn't plan to. But I'm guessing you already figured that out."

"Sorry I —"

"Naw, don't be sorry. There've been too many secrets around here already. My dad wasn't cool the way your parents are."

"Huh?"

"Seriously, letting Zim and me live here? My dad would never."

"What about your mom?"

"She took off when I was little. Really little, I barely remember her."

"Oh. So what about your dad?"

"My dad had, has, a lot of problems. His whole family does. It's kind of a mess. I've been living on my own for a while. I moved out when I was seventeen."

"But how could you afford to, you know, live?"

"I didn't finish high school. I started working as soon as I could to pay my rent. I lived in some really awful places when I was younger."

"Worse than Zim's old apartment?"

"Oh my god, that place was like a palace compared to where I was living."

"Wow."

"Yeah. It was bad. So when I met your brother, I just fell for him right away. He was so different from every other guy I'd known. He's a keeper, your big bro. He's — well, he's a pretty amazing guy."

"Most of the time."

"Yeah." She smiled. "Most of the time."

"Anyway, it made me tough, going through all that," she said. "I may not make all the right decisions.... I mean, I know I've made some bad ones. Tons of them. But somewhere along the way I decided that things, my life, everything, would always work out for the best. I had to, it was all that kept me going. So I figured that if whatever was going on wasn't that great yet, it just meant that I hadn't worked it out. The story wasn't over, you know?"

"Everything always works out for the best?"

"I'm telling you, it helps."

"Maybe."

"Just think about it. Hey, I never told you how much I like your new haircut, did I?" she said.

"Really?"

"Yeah, it definitely suits you."

"Seriously?"

"You bet. But, hey, you still want to help me with my hair?" J pointed to her shaggy bangs, now completely grey.

"Yeah, let's do it."

We went into the bathroom — our poor, over-used, non-spider-ridden bathroom — and J got out Z's electric razor. It was just like the one that Marco had used on the back of my neck at the salon and I got a tiny little jolt of excitement just holding it in my hands.

J put the lid down on the toilet and took a seat. She grabbed the navy towel I'd ruined with zit cream and wrapped it around her neck

"Are you sure about this?" I asked, thinking of the last time that Mom had tried to cut my hair — a complete and total disaster.

"Absolutely. It's impossible to make a mistake with this. Everything must go."

"Everything?"

She smiled.

"Everything."

I plugged the razor in and switched it on. It buzzed to life and I felt another tiny jolt. J solemnly lowered her head and closed her eyes.

To start, I shaved a big fat line down the middle of her head like a reverse mohawk. The back was already pretty short — she'd shaved it a couple of months before, she said — but it was still shocking to see that stripe of J's pale white scalp. From there I kept on buzzing in neat lines, one after the other, like I was mowing a lawn. When we were finished, there was a small pile of pale-pinkish grey and brown hair on the cold tiled floor.

J opened her eyes and looked in the mirror. "It's perfect," she said, turning her head at different angles to get a good look.

"Yeah?"

"Oh yeah."

She went and got our broom and dustpan from the kitchen, swept up the trimmings of her hair, and shook them out into the garbage.

"Jen?" I said, when she was almost finished.

"Uh-huh?"

"I'm glad you're here."

She turned, broom in hand, to totally take me in, and smiled.

Her grin spread slowly across her whole face and she rubbed a hand over her brand-new baldness, shaking loose a few stray hairs onto the floor.

"I'm glad you're here too."

She leaned the broom against the wall and wrapped her arms around me. I squirmed for a second, thinking about her belly as it pressed into me, but she didn't let go. There were tiny bits of stray hair stuck to her neck, and it made my cheek itchy. I didn't mind, though.

SIXTEEN

Slut

From Wikipedia, the free encyclopedia

Slut is a term applied to an individual who is considered to have loose sexual morals or who is sexually promiscuous *or who has been prescribed birth control for a freaking medical condition.* The term is generally pejorative and most often applied to ~~women as an insult or offensive term of disparagement, meaning "dirty or slovenly."~~ *my locker, with a big fat red permanent marker.*

For the second time in two months, it feels like I've died. Only this time I know exactly where I wound up.

Chloe did it. She must have. I'm sure it was her. I tried so hard not to cry when I saw the writing on my locker. It was like each letter was yelling at me, telling me I'd done something wrong, even though I that know I haven't.

And everyone else had seen it too. They were talking about me, I was sure. Making up sick stories. Imagining the worst.

I felt numb. I went to class and told Ms. Vilaney what had happened, and she went out into the hallway to see for herself. She told us all to remain in our seats, but when she walked past mine on her way back in she gave me the dirtiest look.

I wanted to evaporate.

Instead, I just curled up in my chair, trying to make myself as small as possible, which wasn't easy.

Vilaney called for the janitor to come paint over my locker. But the word still screamed at me, still stared at me like a painting with moving eyes in a museum. Even with a classroom wall between us.

And I could tell Vilaney thought it was somehow my fault. The way she looked at me all day, half-afraid and half-fascinated. She was trying to work out what I'd done, maybe even who I'd done it with.

How can I be a slut if no guy will even look at me? It doesn't make sense.

I told Trisha about the Pill.

And Trisha must have told Stacey.

And then Stacey must have told Chloe.

And I know Chloe did it. I know.

I tried so hard all morning not to cry, but ten minutes before lunch I completely cracked. Vilaney sent me off to the bathroom to clean myself up. To wash my face and try to make it look like my eyes weren't as bright red as my cheeks, my zits, the marker, everything.

Trisha tried to come with me to help, but Vilaney said that I was perfectly capable of taking care of myself.

What she meant was that I didn't deserve the help.

Vilaney carried on with her lesson, and I left.

I couldn't believe I'd broken down in class. I cried harder because I was so frustrated at myself for letting it get to me. I wanted so badly to be the girl who was too smart to care about any of this dumb stuff. Like J, knowing people might judge her for what she does, for who she is, but not giving them the satisfaction of feeling bad about herself.

But I'm not Jen. Even with a *funky* haircut.

I can't believe I let Chloe see me cry.

I know I should have called Mom and told her what happened. I almost did. But I knew she would have wanted to call Chloe's parents. And Chloe's parents wouldn't have believed it, they'd have already heard their daughter's perfectly rehearsed alibi.

Nothing's going to happen if I tell. Nothing's going to get better.

It'll just make Chloe angrier, and that would make everything so much worse.

I know Chloe's the one. I'm positive.

But I'm not going to tell.

It'll only make things worse.

Could things actually get any worse?

Is it possible — did Chloe write GINGER, too, on her own locker? Just to stir up trouble?

I can't think about this anymore, it's giving me a headache.

Where's Mom's tomato juice when you need it?

The day finally ended and I got to go home. I've never been so glad to hear the three o'clock bell. I practically ran home, I was so desperate to get out of school and away from everyone. But, when I finally got there, home wasn't relaxing or comforting or even quiet. Everyone was in their own little bubble, totally oblivious to the other soapy spheres in the house, and making a surprising amount of noise.

Dad's bubble was in the basement, the construction site. The *rrrrgh, rrrrgh, rrrrgh* of his power tools had been nearly constant for weeks, even though nothing ever seemed to change down there.

Part of me thinks he's just been hiding out, drinking Rolling Rock from his little cooler, and holding down the trigger on his electric drill.

Z was busy trying to look busy in his bubble, putting on the appearance of a person looking for a job (he isn't — I don't think he'll ever leave that record store), and putting on his music too loud. Very loud. Lots of bass. It practically shook my teeth.

J was totally absorbed in the stack of books she had taken out of the library on pregnancy and babies and what to expect when you're expecting an alien creature to jump out of your womb in seven months' time. She had set herself up at the kitchen table and kept asking

Mom what she thought about all the contradictory advice the books were giving.

The last bubble, Mom, was so wrapped up in cooking that she wasn't hearing half of J's questions, but she was nodding along and trying to throw in as much advice as she could. It didn't help that she had the radio on, tuned to her favourite station, the best of the '60s, '70s, and '80s.

I went up to my room, trying to find a pocket of noiselessness, but the noise was everywhere. There was no escaping the roar of my family. I lay down on my bed, trying to will my headache away, or at least to fall asleep for a few minutes. I closed my eyes and tried to imagine what it would be like to be anyone but me.

I've got another appointment with Dr. Mueller next month, but I'm starting to wonder if I wouldn't be better off just wearing a bag over my head for the rest of my middle-school career.

It might be nice, I could get a different bag for each day of the week and coordinate them with my outfits. Draw a nice big smile on each one so I could save myself the trouble. No one would have to know how miserable I really am.

"Hey," everyone would say, "there goes Bag Girl!"

And I'd smile, even if I was having the world's worst day.

A slut? Really?

How could I be a slut?

SEVENTEEN

Angst

From Wikipedia, the free encyclopedia

Angst means fear or anxiety. The word angst was introduced into English from Danish via existentialist Søren Kierkegaard — *thanks, Kierky.* It is used in English to describe an intense feeling of apprehension, anxiety, or inner turmoil.

Is twelve too young to have teenage angst? My teachers always said I was advanced for my age.

These days, I just want to sleep. I'd be happy if I could sleep all day. I'd sleep all day, and I wouldn't have to go to school, and my family could just keep going on with their lives like I'm not even here. I wouldn't be dead, or anything. But I wouldn't have to keep feeling so awful.

It won't work, though. I drool in my sleep.

As if I needed to look any uglier.

Chloe and Stacey are both officially not speaking to me. Trisha's the one who delivered the news today after school. She kept squirming and fidgeting, which is totally unlike her.

"This is so stupid," she said. "They're being so immature. They think your brother's weird girlfriend is, like, rubbing off on you or something. They say you've been acting …"

I could tell Trisha was trying to think of a nice way to say whatever it is they'd called me.

"Well, different," she said. "I guess since she and Zim moved into your house. The new haircut and stuff. I don't know, I don't get it."

"Right, like they haven't been acting weird too. And the haircut wasn't my fault. I told you, didn't I? It was the weird salon we went to. I didn't mean for it to be so short."

"I know. They think we're not cool enough for them now or something. Ever since Stacey kissed Brad at Maylee's birthday party."

"Since when did Maylee even invite Stacey to her party?" I asked.

Maylee had been in our class for the last two years, but it's not like she ever talked to us brainers. She was definitely cool, and her parties were always a big deal. At her last birthday party she gave out loot bags with twenty-dollar bills in them. At least, that's what I heard.

Maylee existed in a whole other world, one with its own set of laws and customs that were completely foreign to me. I never thought about Maylee and her parties, the same way I never thought about packing up and moving to Kuala Lumpur. It just wasn't going to happen.

"Maylee invited Chloe too," Trisha said. "But the party was like two weeks ago. How is it you haven't heard about this?"

"Because I'm being shunned?"

"Could be. You have been kind of moody lately."

"Hey, I thought you were on my side."

"I am. But your side has been kind of moody lately, no offence."

"Ha ha. So what happened at Maylee's? Stacey really kissed Brad?"

Brad wasn't quite the stereotypical teen movie jock, but he came pretty close. He was on the student government, which I think was mostly because he got to read the morning announcements. You could tell he was in love with his own voice. Like how he stretched out his vowels like he was trying to make each sentence last an hour. No one talks like that unless they've got a microphone in front of them. But Brad played on the basketball team, too. Tall, blond, athletic. Whatever. Total Kuala Lumpurian.

"Yup," Trisha said, "that's it. Stacey wouldn't stop talking about it. It was just some truth or dare thing, but apparently now they're going out or something."

"Whoa."

Stacey had never even kissed a guy before. We used to tell each other everything, and now I was getting the news (her first kiss!) second hand, two weeks after the fact?

"Mm-hmm," Trisha said, "so I guess Stacey's cool now or whatever."

"What about Chloe?"

"Chloe's the one who got them invited to Maylee's. What do you think?"

I'd been noticing that all the time the Linebacker was spending with Stacey was starting to rub off. In the last few months Chloe had started straightening her hair and was wearing more makeup. She'd been dressing more like Stacey, too, many thanks to Hollister and Abercrombie & Fitch. Of course I'd noticed all of these little things, but it hadn't really sunk in.

It all made sense now.

Now that it was too late.

"So where does that leave us?" I asked.

"Band practice?"

"Yeah, I guess so. At least the new cool girls are still speaking to you."

"Barely."

"It's better than nothing."

"I guess," Trisha said.

"You want to come over to my house?"

"You sure Jen's weirdness isn't contagious? I don't think my parents would be too happy if I came home with a shaved head."

"We'll let you keep your locks this time. Besides, Jen's pretty cool. I think you'll like her. She told me she used to be really into Mainline. She's seen them play a couple of times."

Trisha flashed a rare giant smile.

"Okay. I'm in."

We walked to my house, and I was shocked to find it was almost quiet when I put my key in the front door. Mom wasn't home from work yet, and Dad only popped his head up from the basement long enough to tell us that Z was off at a job interview that Old Papa Bear had set up for him. Dad actually called himself that now — how embarrassing. At least he'd quit with the drilling.

I went into the kitchen and grabbed us a snack (some of the tofu jerky that J's been stockpiling in the cupboard — she was craving it like mad last week, but says she can't stand it right of it now) and led Trisha upstairs. J was in her and Z's room down the hall, blasting her music and singing along.

Trisha and I sat on my bed for a while, gnawing on our jerky and listening to J. Her voice wasn't bad. I wondered if she'd ever sung in a band.

"You want to go talk to her?" I asked.

"Think we should?"

"Sure. It's cool. Come on."

I knocked on the bedroom door, even though it was mostly open. We could see J bopping her head to the beat, lightly tapping her belly like it was a drum kit.

"*Entrez!*" J called.

I pushed the door open the rest of the way and we stepped inside. Z's old room was just a little bit bigger than mine, but with all of Z and J's stuff crammed in, it looked about the size of a bathtub. J was sitting at the little desk in the corner with a battered laptop open to Facebook in front of her.

"Hey," I said, "this is my friend Trisha. Trisha, Jen."

"Great to meet you," J said. "You're the Mainline fan, right?"

"Yeah," Trisha said, "I love them."

"Totally," said J. "They put on a great live show."

"Cool."

We all paused for a second, and Trisha caught herself staring at J's stomach. "Sorry, I —" she started to say.

"No biggie," said J, "I'm enormous."

She wasn't at all; she was still only showing a tiny little bit. But J was small to begin with, so I guess she feels like she's really starting to get fat.

"So can you feel the baby at all?" I asked. I'd been kind of curious for a while.

"Sometimes I think I can feel it, but then it turns out to just be gas. Sorry, by the way," J said, fanning the air around her, "that was me."

"Gross," said Trisha.

"Sorry, man," said J, "this is my life."

"Sorry. I didn't mean it like that."

"Ha," said J, "no, no, it's cool. I know I'm not much fun these days. I used to be cool. I think."

"Then you're doing better than we are," I said.

"Speak for yourself," Trisha said.

"Aw, just give it some time," said J. "Smart is cool. It's just going to take a while for everyone else around you to figure that out."

"Like how long?" I asked.

"Definitely by the time you're thirty," J said, smiling huge.

"So, by the time we're old ladies?" Trisha said.

"So helpful," I said.

"I know it's not the advice you want to hear, but just wait. You guys are definitely doing middle school right. Don't waste your time trying to fit in, it's never going to happen. And I mean that as a compliment. A big one."

"Uh huh," I said, "so we're doomed to be outsiders forever?"

"Outsiders Forever, live at the Sound Academy — tickets are completely sold out," said Trisha.

"Nope," I said. "That name'll never work."

"Oh, shoot," Trisha said, looking at the old Mickey Mouse clock hanging on J and Z's wall, "I've got to get home. I'm going to be late for dinner."

"You could eat here," I said, "but I'm pretty sure the only thing in the cupboard right now is rice and beans."

"And you do not want to hang out with a pregnant lady after she's had beans for dinner," J said.

"You guys are weird," said Trisha.

"We'll take that as a compliment," said J.

"You mind if I use your bathroom to change?"

"Why do you need to change?" J said. "Those outer-space leggings are amazing."

Trisha contemplated her legs, which were covered in miniature galaxies. "I know. But these are kind of just for me, you know? They're like a secret."

"Are your parents, like, really strict?" J asked.

"They're all right."

"So why keep it a secret?"

133

"I don't know," Trisha said, suddenly looking bashful. "I guess I'm still figuring it out."

J and I nodded, and Trisha took her bag from my room to change back into a slightly less stellar (get it?) outfit.

I walked with Trisha back downstairs and gave her a hug as she left. Trisha's not much of a hugger, but it felt right, even if we were both a little awkward about it.

"Thanks," I said, as we broke apart.

"For what?"

"For being the only person in my life who hasn't completely changed who they are this year."

"I told you," Trisha said, "there's no way my parents would let me shave my head."

"How do you do it? Just stay so calm about everything."

"My dreams of rock and roll superstardom keep me grounded."

"Guess it's about time I actually learned some chords then, huh?"

"Obviously. No one would pay to see only one Slush Puppy."

"See? I knew you liked it!"

"It has a certain ring to it."

"See you later, Slush Pup."

"Don't ever call me that again." Trisha's thin little grin betrayed her fake toughness.

"Since when did you become a hugger, anyway?"

"Oh, you know, just practising for our adoring fans."

I waved at her through the living room window as she walked home.

Mom came home not long after that and started making dinner. J and I set the table, and Dad and informed us that the basement was starting to look like an apartment — he'd have it ready for Z and J in a few days.

"Maybe it's time I quit my job and hired myself out as a contractor," he said.

"Thanks so much for all the work you've done," J said. "It means, well, it means a lot that you guys have been so welcoming to me."

Mom smiled nervously. "Of course, dear," she said. "You're family now."

"You bet," said Dad.

"Duh," I said.

J reached over and tousled my hair. "Thanks, guys."

I grinned.

It was almost seven and Z still hadn't come back from his job interview.

"Should we wait?" J asked.

"Best to eat this stuff while it's still hot," Dad said. "I'm sure Zim won't mind."

So the four of us dug into our mountains of kidney, navy, and fava. None of us said much. We'd almost cleared our plates when we finally heard Z at the door. J got up to greet him.

"Hungry, Zim?" Mom asked.

"Nah," he said, "I think I'm just going to head upstairs."

"Come on," said Dad, "sit down. Tell us about the interview."

J came back to the table and sat down, but Z just hovered near the empty chair Dad pulled up for him.

"What was the job?" I asked.

"My old buddy Bill was looking for an assistant manager for his store," Dad said. "He sells electronics, and I told him our Zim was a retail genius looking for a new challenge. So, tell us how it went, Zed."

"Fine," Z said, refusing to sit. "It went okay. I'm just tired. I think I'm going to go to bed."

"What's wrong, hon?" Mom asked, returning from the kitchen with a fifth plate of beans.

"I just don't think it's the job for me," Z said. "I don't think it would be a good fit."

"Come on, Bill's a great guy. I'm sure he'd be a decent boss. What, did you make a bad impression?" Dad asked.

Z's eyes scanned from Dad to Mom before resting on J. "I didn't go," he said quietly.

"What do you mean?" J asked.

"I mean I didn't go to the interview. I didn't go see Bill. I'm not going to take the job. I didn't go."

Dad's not usually an angry person, but in that moment you'd never have known it. Mom mostly just looked sad and drained. So did J.

No one spoke. So I did. "What are you going to do now?"

"I'm going to keep working at the record store," Z said.

"And when the baby's born?" Dad asked.

"It's a good job, Dad. They care about me there, and they're going to support me, us, however they can. I think they're finally going to give me some day shifts, too, so it'll be all right."

"You've done some dumb things in your life, Zim," Dad said, fighting to keep his voice calm, "and I should know, because I've done some of those things too. But you not taking responsibility for your child is by far the dumbest thing I've seen you do. And I'm not going to sit by and watch you become a negligent parent, all right? I'm not. You're going to call Bill and beg him to give you another chance. I don't know if he'll give it to you, but you sure as ... well, anyway, you better get down on your knees and try."

"I'm not doing it," Z said.

"You're not," said Dad in disbelief.

"I'm going to find another job eventually, okay? But for now I think I'm good where I am."

"Oh?" said Dad.

"I mean, you say you've done the stuff I've done, you've made bad choices or whatever so you understand, but then you won't let me choose how to support my family."

"If I thought you could find a decent job on your own, I'd be happy to let you. But you've been doing nothing but waste time since you've moved back home, and I think you've made a huge mistake." He reached out and put his hand over J's on the table. "I'm sorry," he said.

"Oh yeah?" said Z, "Because you've never made a mistake? Never had a kid without planning for it? Never imagined your whole life would go differently only to have everything change in a second? It's not like you guys exactly planned for Jo."

"Planned for me to what?" I said. And then, of course, it hit me.

From the very first moment, I was a mistake.

EIGHTEEN

Unintended pregnancy

From Wikipedia, the free encyclopedia

Unintended pregnancies include unwanted pregnancies as well as those that are mistimed.

> *Unintended pregnancies include Jen's (2012) as well as my mom's (1999). Side effects of unintended pregnancies include heartburn, nausea, and unintended babies.*
>
> *Unintended babies may grow up to be hideous, angsty people with few friends and fewer boyfriends.*
>
> *Unintended babies may also resent being born into such a family and the world in general.*

Jo Waller, unintended child.

Jo Waller, pockmarked and unlovable.

Jo Waller, listening to one of stupid Z's stupidly excellent mixes on her iPod with the volume up full blast, not listening to you.

First, Mom knocked on the door.

"Go away!" I yelled.

But she came in anyway.

She told me how much she and my dad loved me.

How hard she knows that things have been for me.

How yes, it's true, she hadn't planned for me to happen, but that she had always, always wanted a daughter.

How she had thought that she was just too old to have any more kids so that when I came along it was like magic. And she was so glad.

She couldn't have planned a better kid, she said. And that's the way the world works — some of the greatest things that have ever happened were never planned, were somehow magic. She said.

I tried to smother myself with a pillow until, eventually, she left.

Dad came in next. He said most of the same things Mom did. That he loved me, and that I was special. That Z was an idiot. That Z was a huge idiot. That if he could choose to have had just one kid it would be me, because I was not an idiot (I think he was trying to make a joke, but he was still pretty mad so it wasn't really funny).

And then Z sat down on my bed. And Dad left pretty quick.

"I'm so sorry, Jo," Z said. "I'm an idiot, you know that?"

"Dad mentioned it," I said, my voice muffled by the pillow I was still half-heartedly attempting to suffocate myself with.

Z picked the pillow up off my face and he could see that I'd been crying. "I mean it. I'm the worst brother ever."

"That was so mean." My voice was tiny and far away.

"I know."

"Why would you say that?" I wiped my nose with the back of my hand.

"Because I was angry. And I'm scared. And because I'm an idiot, okay? Your brother is an idiot."

"Yeah."

"And I know you'll never forgive me, but I've still got to try. I could …"

His voice trailed off, thinking.

I refused to help him out. I absolutely couldn't believe that he'd said what he said. I don't care how mad he was or how much he had to get Dad off his back, or even how scared he was about the baby. It was the worst thing anyone had ever said about me. The worst.

And Z didn't know me at all, really. How could he even know that I'd been an accident? He'd been gone since I was six years-old. Seeing me once every couple of weeks for a family dinner wasn't the same as being a real big brother. He had no right to say anything about me. I couldn't believe I'd idolized him for so long. He was lazy, he was stupid, and his poor kid wasn't going to stand a chance. His kid was a mistake. A huge mistake.

"Guitar," Z said finally, breaking the silence. "I could teach you how to play the guitar, for real."

"You said that before. And then you didn't. You never keep your promises."

"Then I'm going to start. And the first thing I'm going to do is teach you to play. Right now, I'll go get my guitar."

"Not tonight."

"Okay, tomorrow?"

"You promise?" I said, finally sitting up.

"Absolutely."

"You mean it?"

"I'm trying," he said.

"You should take that job."

"No, Jo, I shouldn't. This is something I'm going to have to figure out for myself."

"It can't be that bad. You have to try. Promise you'll try to get another interview."

"I'm not going to do that."

"Promise. Promise you'll try or I'll never forgive you."

"You drive a hard bargain, little sis." He smiled. "But I'm not going to beg for another interview. That's not what I'd want my kid to do."

"Then your kid's going to be a loser like you."

"Ouch." The smile disappeared. "Okay. I deserved that."

"Yeah, you did."

"How about I make you another promise? A different one."

"Like what?"

"Like if I promise to be the best father in the world to that amazing little baby Jen's carrying — if I'm the greatest dad ever, then will you forgive me?"

"I'll think about it."

"That sounds about right," Z said, getting up. "I'll see you tomorrow for our first lesson."

"Whatever. Shut the door, okay?"

But a couple of minutes later, there was one more knock.

"Go away, Zim!" I yelled, "I'm not forgiving you tonight."

"Sorry, Jo," said J, "we can talk another time."

"Oh. No, it's okay, you can come in for a minute."

I was back down on my bed, lying starfish, face down, but I sat up when J closed the door behind her and I made space for her on the bed. She sat cross-legged facing me.

"I want you to know that I'm totally pissed at your brother," she said.

"Good."

"He had no right to say what he said. He better have been grovelling when he was in here. Did he grovel? Was there grovelling?"

"Not exactly. But he's going to teach me guitar."

"Geez, you'll be friggin' Jimmy Page by the time he's racked up enough lesson credits to earn back your trust."

"Uh-huh," I said, even though I wasn't totally sure who Jimmy Page was.

"Anyway," J said, "I just wanted you to know how important you are to me. It's been … it's been tough moving in here with your parents, and I know it's been hard on them, too, having me around. None of us planned for this to happen, but I've never regretted it for a second."

I tried to keep my face from looking totally skeptical, but J could see I wasn't buying it.

"What I mean is, I never would have guessed that this would happen to me, but I can't wait to meet this new person that Zim and I are going to be bringing into the world."

"It's crazy," I said. "Um, I mean —" thinking about what J had said about her family.

"No, you're right. It's completely, unbelievably bananas. And it's going to be hard, I know it is. And I feel so ridiculously lucky to have your family around to support us."

"Really?"

"Of course. This kid is going to have more love than it'll know what to do with. Plus it's going to have the coolest aunt ever."

"Doubtful."

"You're amazing, Jo. And as a not-yet member of your family, I can say that with total objectivity. Being twelve sucks, but you're going to be all right. You are so, so lucky."

"Yeah right," I said, framing my inflamed cheeks like a game show model.

"I said being twelve sucked, didn't I?"

"Uh-huh." I smiled. "I think you're lucky too, Jen."

"I think you're right," J said, running a hand over her belly.

"You still believe that everything works out for the best?"

"Yup. Definitely."

That night I wrote a letter, a real one, not an email.

I wrote about all the horrible things I'd been feeling, about how bad it felt having a friend turn on me, and about losing another friend, a best friend, in the process. I wrote about how I don't even care about being cool, I just want to be cool with myself.

I erased that last bit, then. It sounded too cheesy.

In the letter I explained that being on birth control doesn't make me a slut, that no one should be called a slut, that the word is incredibly hateful. I explained that the colour of someone's hair — or their skin, or anything — doesn't give anyone the right to make fun of them either. And that I absolutely did not write anything on anyone's locker at school. I didn't. But I'm sorry it happened and I know what it's like to feel like you don't count.

I wrote about how excited I was to be learning to play guitar, and that I really meant it about starting a band. That there were people just like me out there, musicians and artists and total circus freaks, and I couldn't wait to meet them. The band, the music, was going to be a way of sticking out my hand and saying hi to my fellow losers. Hopefully, anyway. And I couldn't wait.

Because smart and weird may not be cool right now, but it will be. One day.

And because everything always works out for the best in this giant work-in-progress.

I believe that now, I wrote.

And I signed my name at the bottom of the letter. And I folded it up and I put it in an envelope that I found in the one of the junk drawers in the kitchen. I licked the glue on the flap at the top and I sealed it.

And on the front of the envelope I wrote her name. Chloe.

The next day at school I showed up early.

I walked the four blocks with purpose. It was a warm day for March, and I left my coat unzipped.

I was early. Really early.

But so was a kid in grade eight who I'd seen around school before but had never talked to, I didn't even know his name. He was the only other person in the hallway at eight-thirty, and he turned when he heard my footsteps. He looked me like I was a monster, a dragon, a grizzly bear. He dropped the marker he was holding — red — and ran.

I stopped dead.

It was him? Seriously? Some weasely prankster too afraid to even speak?

I was stunned.

It hadn't been Chloe at all. How was that possible? It was just some random vandal.

Why had he done this to us? Did he have any idea what trouble he'd caused?

I took a deep breath, and then another one. My chest felt suddenly light.

I walked over to the locker where he'd been standing — I recognized it right away, it belonged to a guy in my class named Scotty, a total goof who thought it was funny that his locker number was 666 — and read what he'd written.

FREA

I'd spotted him just in time. Before he could make someone else feel like a freak.

But it made no sense.

Scotty's not a freak. He's on the basketball team. He has friends, too, lots of friends.

But the attack on Chloe's locker obviously wasn't random.

So maybe someone — this idiot grade eight with a Sharpie and whoever his friends were — knew about me being on the Pill.

Or maybe they didn't.

Was it a just a coincidence or was it a cruel joke?

I had no idea.

And not knowing didn't make me feel any better, but it did make me feel different.

I tore open the envelope and reread my letter to Chloe, wondering if I still wanted her to see it now that I knew she hadn't been the guilty one.

I dug around in my backpack for a pen, and, at the bottom on the letter wrote:

I know you didn't do it either. The locker.

But that was never what this was all about, was it?

I opened my locker and took out all the things I needed for the day, then locked it and walked toward the gym.

I taped the envelope up again, and slid it into Chloe's new locker — it was the one next to Stacey's, still covered in ribbons and wrapping paper and magazine clippings from her birthday — through the grate at the top. I left the set of glasses — the not quite replacement replacements that I'd almost forgotten about in my locker — sitting just in front.

And I walked towards the principal's office, red marker in hand.

I didn't know if they'd believe me, or what this random creep's punishment might be. I knew telling wouldn't put the earth back on its axis. And probably neither would the letter. But it might be a start.

NINETEEN

Fallout (disambiguation)

From Wikipedia, the free encyclopedia

Nuclear fallout is the residual radiation hazard from a nuclear explosion.

Fallout or fall-out may also refer to:

Music

- Fallout (heavy metal band), a short-lived (1979–1982) Brooklyn-based heavy metal band

Television

- "Fallout" (*Stargate SG-1*), a 2004 episode of the television series *Stargate SG-1*

Other

- *Fallout* (video game), a 1997 post-apocalyptic computer role-playing game released by Interplay Entertainment
- *What happens when you drop a bombshell letter and hope that everything will eventually get back to maybe-normal and it doesn't.*
- *But maybe that's okay.*

In the movie version of my life I could have left the letter — and the glasses, my peace offering — and just walked off into the sunset or whatever, knowing that everything was going to be fine forever. That maybe Chloe and Stacey and I wouldn't be such great friends anymore, but that Stacey and I would always keep in touch because we were so close for so long.

That isn't how it happened, though.

I couldn't stop thinking about Chloe reading the letter. Chloe probably laughing at me for being a baby, but trying to act so grown up. Chloe showing the letter to Stacey to make fun of me. But what did Stacey think of it?

Chloe and Stacey spent a couple of days avoiding me, so while it was hard to tell what exactly they thought of the letter, it was pretty obvious that it was nothing good.

It made my stomach hurt — it kept twisting itself in tighter and tighter knots while I waited to see what would happen. Would they write their own letter? Would they never speak to me again? It wasn't that I regretted writing the letter, but the waiting afterwards was almost worse than everything that had come before. Almost, but not quite.

Z and J took me out for pizza one night when they saw how upset I was. And, actually, it was great. They even let me bring Trisha.

We all took the subway, since Z still can't drive on his own, and went downtown — a neighbourhood called Little Portugal — to this really cool place that serves the thinnest pizza you've ever seen, with toppings you'd never even think to put on a pizza. Pear? Duck? Seriously?

The menu looked kind of expensive, but Z told me it was okay — that he and J were friends with a few of the servers, and they'd probably cut a few bucks off our bill, as long as we tipped well. J said she'd been craving this pizza for months, and that a bad day was the best reason she could think of for us all to stuff ourselves with deliciousness.

I told them about writing the letter. And about the nervous feeling in my stomach while I waited for the world to end or maybe not. I told them about our lockers too, and the grade eight guy with the marker.

"Wow," J said, taking a sip from her water glass that she kept refilling every two minutes like she was on a long trek through the desert, "that was brave, Jo. Seriously."

"Yeah," said Z, "totally. But it's going to suck for a while, you know that, right?"

"I kind of figured that out the hard way," I said, my stomach gurgling in anticipation of pizza with buffalo mozzarella — who knew you could even milk a buffalo?

"It's definitely going to suck," said Trisha.

She'd told me privately that she kind of hated that I'd written the letter. She understood why I'd done it, but I guess I hadn't realized that it would make things weird for her, too.

"Yeah, sorry about that," I said.

Fortunately, she hadn't been too mad. Which was good, or else I would have been down to no friends at all. Except Z and J.

"It's fine," said Trisha, taking a piece of bread from the basket in front of us and swirling it in a plate of olive oil and balsamic vinegar.

"Yup," J said, grabbing some bread, too, "or it will be. You know, eventually."

"And what happened with that random with the marker?" Z asked. "Did they, like, suspend him or whatever?"

"No, but he got in pretty big trouble. I'm not totally sure what happened."

"That's so weird," said J.

"Uh-huh. Part of me wonders if we'd all still be friends if this guy hadn't messed with us for no reason."

"I don't know," Trisha said through a mouthful of oily bread. "I kind of think it would've happened anyway."

"Yeah, maybe," I said, gulping back my water. I knew Trisha was probably right, but it still kind of hurt.

And even though I still felt sad — and weird that I was maybe never going to be real friends with Stacey again — it was a pretty great night. It wasn't quite what Zim had promised me more than a year ago; we definitely weren't going to stay up and see the sunrise or even wander around the neighbourhood together (Mom and Dad had told us we had to be home by ten), but it was still great.

Our pizzas arrived and were unbelievably good. If I lived downtown I think I'd eat that stuff at least once a week — and my face would never recover. But just as Z and J were settling up the bill with our server — and by settling up I mean laughing and trading stories while our server, a friend of theirs, felt J's belly — I spotted a familiar face entering the restaurant.

Declan. Walsh.

With his parents!

Somehow I'd imagined that Declan's whole family would be perfectly cool. Like they were some alien race of absolutely calm, chill people, who also happened to be amazing guitar players — his talent had to come from somewhere, right?

But Declan's mom and dad looked more like scatterbrained professors. His dad's hair was grey and curly, but with a seriously pronounced bald spot in the middle, and his mom was wearing about fifteen different brightly coloured scarves around her neck. They were laughing about something while Declan looked kind of annoyed to be seen somewhere so hip with his parents who so obviously weren't.

"That's him," I whispered to Trisha, trying to subtly nod my head in Declan's direction.

"Who?" Trisha said, surveying the dining room.

"Stop it," I hissed, "don't be so obvious. That guy over there with his parents. It's *Declan*."

"Wow," Trisha said, copping a not-so-subtle stare, "he's cute."

"Isn't he?"

But before I could think of what I could possibly say to him, Z and J had their coats on, and told us we'd better be getting back.

I slowly zipped up my coat, drinking Declan in from the corner of my vision. He was cute — almost impossibly cute — but he really was just a guy. A guy who ate pizza. A guy who was embarrassed to be seen out in public with his parents.

I trailed just a little ways behind Z, J, and Trisha as we walked out of the restaurant, and paused by Declan's table as I passed it.

His parents were deep into the menu, but Declan was staring at the far wall, looking bored. He caught my eye and I held my breath.

"Hey," he said.

"Hey." It came out of my mouth like a puff of smoke, and I smiled. "You should try the buffalo mozzarella. It's good."

He smiled back at me. "Cool."

Which is when my heart basically gave out under me and I ran to catch up with the others.

"What happened?" Trisha whispered to me as we walked towards the bus stop to take us back to the subway. J and Z were ahead of us, talking about cribs or something.

"He said hey." My voice was dreamy and disbelieving.

"Yeah?" Trisha said, obviously impressed.

"Yeah."

I put my arm through hers, squeezing us together to try to block out the freezing wind, and we walked to the bus stop together.

TWENTY

Wedding (disambiguation)

From Wikipedia, the free encyclopedia

A wedding is the ceremony in which two people are united in marriage or a similar institution *like, "Well, I guess if we love each other and we're having a baby, we might as well make it official."* Wedding traditions and customs vary greatly between cultures, ethnic groups, religions, countries, and social classes. Most wedding ceremonies involve an exchange of wedding vows by the couple *which, if you're J and Z, you will write yourselves and they will be so sweet and funny that you will actually make each other crack up and cry during the ceremony*, presentation of a gift (offering, rings, symbolic item, flowers, money, *matching tattoos — seriously, I couldn't make this up, they each got rings tattooed on their fingers*), and a public proclamation of marriage by an authority figure or leader — *or whoever that woman at city hall was.* Special wedding garments are often worn *(J and Z actually bought their wedding clothes at Value Village — it was ridiculous, and pretty excellent. J managed to find a puffy white dress that fit over her belly, and I wore an old lacy prom dress that she promised looked cool. Z wore a ruffled shirt and suspenders and looked kind of like a magician)* and the ceremony is sometimes followed by a wedding reception *a.k.a. a giant party in our tiny, tiny house.* Music, poetry, prayers, or readings from religious texts or literature are also commonly incorporated into the ceremony — *or, if you're anything like these guys, the whole thing will be done to the tunes of AC/DC.*

I almost couldn't believe it when Z proposed to J, even though I think Mom and Dad saw it coming. He did it while we were all out for dinner for my birthday. He definitely stole the spotlight, but I didn't mind at all.

Well, maybe I did mind just a little.

But the wedding was great, and we had so much fun. There was a ton of music and food at the house afterwards, and lots of people came. Z and J's friends were there, but so were Mom and Dad's. I invited Stacey just because it still kind of felt like she should be there, even though we hadn't really talked since the letter. But her family was going out of town that weekend, so she couldn't make it. Or anyway, that's what she said. It kind of hurt, but not as much as I thought it would. Trisha came, though, and we danced like mad together and had an amazing time. Some of Z and J's musician friends even brought their instruments and played a mini concert in the basement. Now *that* was cool.

But I guess we're not going to be able to party like that for a while because we'll be too busy baby-proofing the house for Z and J's kid.

A girl — they just found out.

I'm going to be an amazing aunt to a tough, smart, beautiful little girl.

The photographer we hired for the wedding — one of J's friends from the bookstore — didn't do such a great job. A lot of the pictures were weird and shaky, but there's one she took that I absolutely love.

It's of me and J and Trisha dancing, but it's only a picture of our feet. Trisha's wearing Mary Janes and a skirt with red-and-black striped tights, and you can just see the bottom of her shirt, a Mainline concert tee that J gave her when her belly outgrew it (the plain clothes Trisha had left her house in were lying somewhere on my bedroom floor — she wasn't ready to stop being a secret superhero/rock star just yet). J and I are still wearing our big, poofy dresses from the ceremony. We're holding up the skirts so we can dance properly, and you can see two sets of hands holding fistfuls of tulle, and, underneath them, two sets of combat boots dancing for their lives.

ACKNOWLEDGEMENTS

Thank you to the staff and patrons of the Toronto Public Library's Parkdale branch, where I furiously typed out the first draft of my manuscript during an only slightly terrifying stretch of unemployment.

Thank you to Mandy Sherman, that first draft's first editor. And to Sheila Barry for further notes and encouragement that eventually whipped *Something Wiki* into shape. Thanks for the job, too.

Thank you to Shannon Whibbs for her energy and editorial flair that helped polish the story and brought it to life as an honest-to-dorkness book.

Thank you to my family and friends for their bottomless pit of love and support.

And thank you to Graham — and Ramona — for giving me the best possible place to come home to.